MURDERED GODS

MARINA FINLAYSON

FINESSE SOLUTIONS

Cover design by Karri Klawiter
Model stock image from Taria Reed/The Reed Files
Editing by Larks & Katydids
Formatting by Polgarus Studio

Published by Finesse Solutions Pty Ltd
2016/12/#01

Author's note: This book was written and produced in Australia and
uses British/Australian spelling conventions, such as "colour" instead
of "color", and "-ise" endings instead of "-ize" on words like "realise".

National Library of Australia Cataloguing-in-Publication entry:

Finlayson, Marina, author.
Murdered gods / Marina Finlayson.
ISBN 9780994239181 (paperback)
Finlayson, Marina. Shadows of the Immortals; bk. 1.
Fantasy fiction.

For Connor and Jen. Thanks for all the plalks.

1

It's not every day you have a beer with the Lord of the Underworld. I'd shared drinks with him before, but that was when I thought he was a vampire named Alberto Alinari. Today he'd revealed, in spectacular fashion, that underneath the undead exterior he was actually Hades, king of the dead.

I was surprisingly unfazed by this discovery. What can I say? It had been a rough couple of days. Stealing magic rings out from under the nose of the most powerful fireshaper in the land, statues coming to life, betrayals and counter-betrayals ... yeah, it had been a busy week. And we weren't done yet.

The beer was cold, and most welcome after the *oh-my-God-I'm-about-to-die* stress of the fight outside. The wet glass left damp rings on the shining wood of the bar. It wasn't like Alberto—excuse me, Lord Hades—to forget the

1

coaster, but I guess it had been a stressful morning for him, too, what with saving us from imminent death, just in the nick of time. Alberto always had been one for the big, showy gesture.

"You going to drink that, or just push it around in circles?" the Lord of the Underworld asked in a rather testy tone. He was most particular about the pristine surface of his bar, which he usually kept polished to a shine you could see your face in.

I picked up my glass and chugged the beer, the amber liquid sliding down my parched throat, then slammed the empty glass back down on the bar. "Drink it."

He raised one perfectly arched eyebrow. I'd always thought he looked like the stereotype of a vampire—dark hair swept back from a pale, high forehead, with a certain air of elegance in his clothes and manner. Now I wondered if he really looked like that at all.

"Another?" he asked.

"Please." I watched him refill the glass, then rather pointedly wipe the bar clean of wet spots. "Unless you've got some ambrosia back there."

"It's overrated." He poured some milk into a saucer and set it beside the beer. Syl leapt up onto the bar and lapped daintily at it. "Fine if you've got a thing for liquid honey, otherwise you'd probably find it too sweet."

"I can't believe we're having this conversation."

Me either, Syl said into my mind, her pink tongue carefully cleaning drops of milk from her whiskers. *Ask him what Hell's like.*

If you stayed human for more than two minutes at a time, you could ask him yourself. I'd seen her human form twice in the last twenty-four hours, and that was twice more than I had in the whole of the last three months. Surely now that Anders was dead she didn't feel the need to hide the fact that she was a shifter any more?

The whole situation was surreal. The shapers' gods—who I'd never believed in—were not only real in a vague, watching-over-us kind of way, but actually physically present in the world, and taking part in the action. As if it wasn't bad enough to be mixed up with the shapers themselves, without throwing divinities into the mix.

"Why have you been pretending to be a vampire running a pub in the middle of nowhere if you're actually a—a god?" I could hardly even say it. Already, the proof was growing hazy in my memory, as if my mind were trying to protect me from the knowledge. Had I really seen him surrounded by swirling shadows? Driving his hand into a man's chest, killing with his touch?

"Eternity is a long time." Alberto's dark eyes watched me intently, though he lounged against the other side of the bar, apparently relaxed. "I've been many things, and lived many places. After the first millennium or so even a god

3

gets tired of adulation, and anonymity starts looking really attractive. Celebrity isn't all it's cracked up to be, you know."

"So you decided to try life as a vampire bartender?"

He shrugged. "Why not? I've been worse things. Besides, in times like these, it pays to keep your head down."

"Times like what?"

"Times when humans get it into their heads to start killing gods and stealing their powers."

"That doesn't make any sense. How can you be killed if you're immortal?"

He sighed. "Oh, trust me, there are ways. And 'immortal' is a human interpretation, anyway. An easy word for a difficult concept. From a human perspective, 'immortal' is as good a word as any. At any rate, the shadow shapers don't seem to be having any trouble. In the last year, my underworld has been flooded with gods, all turning up looking absolutely stunned to find themselves dead. It's practically a war, but one we don't have any idea how to fight."

I thought those ancient Greek guys were all about the fighting? Syl said. *Well, that, and the sex. Every second story had Zeus bonking someone else.*

"Why not?" I asked, doing my best to ignore Syl's commentary. Hades probably wouldn't appreciate my

4

sniggering while we were discussing something so serious. I shot Syl a dirty look, but she blinked those big, green eyes innocently.

"We're a suspicious lot," he said. "We've had to be, to survive this long. We all have our ways of protecting ourselves. Yet somehow these shadow shapers are getting through our defences, capturing even the mightiest of us. People who ought not to be vulnerable. No one knows how they're doing it." He sighed. "Which of course makes everyone even less trusting. Honestly, trying to get gods to work together is like herding cats. No offence, Syl."

She stuck a haughty pink nose in the air. *I don't see why people have to pick on cats for their metaphors. It's not like herding* anything *is exactly easy, is it?*

"So you're hiding out here?" I certainly had been. Berkley's Bay was a great place for it: quiet, with a large transient population.

His saturnine brows drew together into a frown. Oops. Maybe gods didn't like suggestions of cowardice. "I've been here for years, since long before this trouble started. Let's just say, anonymity is *particularly* attractive right now."

So, definitely hiding, then. I didn't know why he couldn't just admit it. If it was true that the shadow shapers had some secret way of sneaking up on the gods, or whatever they were doing, there was no shame in wanting to stay hidden safely away.

I looked around the bar, which was not as dark as it normally would be at this time of day. The building had no windows, since vampires and daylight don't get along so well. Two sets of doors stood between the interior and the street outside, with a small space in between, like the airlock in a spacecraft. Alberto the vampire had always been very particular about making sure the clientele only opened one door at a time, to stop the light from entering.

Now the inner doors hung crazily from their hinges, and the outer doors were gone, having been blasted into the street when Alberto had joined the fight outside. Bright morning sunshine stretched in a long golden stripe across the patterned carpet and threw the floral carvings on the front of the bar into relief.

"So what are you going to do now?" I gestured at the light, and the broken doors. "Everyone will know you're not a vampire, as soon as word spreads." If the shadow shapers got wind of what he'd done, how long would he stay hidden? "Will you stay?"

"Will word spread?"

He's kidding, right? said Syl. *Has he met Tegan?*

Tegan was the weretiger who ran the hair salon right next to my bookshop. Like most hairdressers, she had an easy way of chatting with her clients. If you wanted to know what was happening in Berkley's Bay, Tegan's salon was the first place you went. Tegan had taken one look at Jake, covered in blood and practically incoherent with exhaustion, and bundled him into her car.

"Tegan will be at the hospital by now. And if everyone in the place hasn't heard the story within the next half hour, I'll die of shock."

Alberto smiled. Hades smiled? Dammit, I couldn't think of him as Hades. For the last three months, I'd known him as Alberto, my employer and benefactor. And now, apparently, my very own *deus ex machina*. "Tegan will have forgotten the more troubling aspects of our little drama by the time she reaches the hospital."

"She will?" It took my brain a moment to catch up. God, I was tired. I'd been awake for over twenty-four hours, most of them under high stress. "You mean you've … magicked her to forget?"

"In a manner of speaking. I *am* the master of the underworld and all it contains." When I continued to stare blankly, he added pointedly, "Including the Lethe, river of forgetting."

Cool, said Syl. *Magic mindpowers.*

"What about the others who saw?"

"All taken care of, though there weren't as many witnesses as you seem to think. People tend to duck for cover when shapers duke it out."

True. The street had cleared faster than a one-legged man in a butt-kicking competition once Jake and Anders had started lobbing fireballs at each other.

"And what about me?" I glanced down at my beer with sudden suspicion. "Am I going to forget too?"

"Do you want to?"

Did I? Did I want to forget that wild ride in the car, with Holly snarling at me in her wolf form? Did I want to forget the moment her baby had slithered into my hands, slippery with blood and birth fluids? Or the moment Jake had thrown himself in front of me to save me from Anders?

"I think I want to see Jake."

He was a fireshaper, just like Anders, the man who'd tried to kill me. I should have hated him, but other, more difficult feelings kept bubbling to the surface. Hate was easy. Acceptance was the real challenge. I wasn't ready to think beyond that, however cute his shaper arse looked in tight jeans, or whatever his molten blue gaze did to my insides.

I drained the last of my beer and slid off the bar stool.

"Before you go—" Alberto's pale hand caught at my wrist. His flesh was cool, and I felt sure that if I had touched my fingers to his pulse points I wouldn't have found a heartbeat. The vampire illusion was compelling. "Tell me about this ring Anders sent you to steal. Where is it now?" His voice was still light, as if he spoke of something of no consequence, but the pressure of his fingers was firm. This ring was important. But then, I already knew that.

"Jake had it in his pocket," I said, meeting his gaze squarely.

That was true. Jake *had* had it in his pocket. Right up until I slipped it out while he was unconscious and snuck it into my own. It rested there still, pressed against my hip bone. If Alberto had looked down, he would have seen the slight bulge it made in the smooth line of my jeans.

His face paled, though a moment before I would have said that was impossible. "Jake has it?" It was a ring of power; I knew that much. People had already died for it. But it was what I didn't know about it that had led me to … acquire it. "Then I'll accompany you to the hospital. If it's what I think it is …"

Now that could get awkward. Darkness swirled about him like a cloak and I glanced uneasily toward the door. What was the big deal with this ring? Seemed like every man and his dog wanted to get their hands on the thing. Anders had called it the "avatar of Apollo". And here was a god, one of Apollo's kin. Who better to take charge of such a dangerous object? The sensible thing to do would be to give it to him and be shot of it. Who wanted to make an enemy of a god?

"Actually, I think I might go home and shower first before I head over to the hospital." I forced my hand not to stray in the direction of my pocket. Sensible be damned. That ring had *whispered* to me, as if it were alive, when I'd first slid it onto my finger. If I was going crazy, I at least had to know *why*. "I'll meet you there."

His gaze took in my blood-spattered appearance. Very little of the blood was mine, but I wasn't a pretty sight. "Not a bad idea. They'll think they have another patient if you go in looking like that. Don't be long."

He strode out into the bright morning sun. He'd have to fritz a few more people's memories if he insisted on wandering around in broad daylight like that. This ring must be super important to him. It had certainly been important to Anders—enough for him to kill to get it. What did a shaper want with a god's ring? Everyone seemed to want it, from Hades to Jake and the rest of the Ruby Council. What was the big deal with it? And if it was Apollo's ring, where was Apollo?

Syl stalked along the bar and sat herself down directly in front of me. *All right, what aren't you telling me?*

For a moment, I considered lying to her, but Syl was my best friend. If I was going to do a runner, she at least deserved to know the truth. I pulled the ring out and laid it on the bar.

Oh, shit, she said. *You didn't.*

"I did."

It was a showy piece; a golden sun, with stylised rays spiralling off it. She laid one delicate black paw on it. *I was afraid of that, when you said* Jake had it *like that. Do you think gods can tell if you lie to them?*

"How should I know? I've never met any before."

Please tell me we aren't giving this back to the Ruby Adept.

"Of course not."

Then what are we doing with it?

"*We* aren't doing anything with it. *I'm* taking it back to Newport." Back to the city of my birth, to the mother who'd told me never to return.

You're going back there? What for?

I swiped the ring off the bar and shoved it back in my pocket. "I need some answers. About me. About my father. And especially about this ring."

Every time I touched it, I could feel the damn thing calling to me, like a telephone line with a really bad connection. It felt like if I only concentrated a little harder I'd be able to make out what it was saying.

And that was freaking me out. Was I going crazy? Maybe madness ran in the family line. I had to know.

I'll come with you, Syl said. The little black cat stared up at me, green eyes unblinking.

"You can't. You're a shifter. They don't take too kindly to those in the human territories."

Then I'll be your pet cat. No one has to know.

I strode out of the pub, with her trotting at my heels, her anxious face turned up to me. "Turn human, and you can come."

I'm happy the way I am, thank you.

I snorted. Happy? She was too frightened to come out of her cat form—she just wouldn't admit it. "Anders is dead. What are you afraid of now?"

Nothing. I just like being a cat.

"It's not normal, Syl. No one stays in their animal shape forever."

Sure they do.

"Okay, nobody who wants to stay sane, then." I unlocked the door to our apartment and she brushed past me. "You have to come out of there before you forget how to be human."

Her tail twitched angrily. *Don't tell me what I have to do. You're not a shifter! I'm a cat and I'll bloody well be a cat if I want to. Now shut up and pack. I'm coming with you, you ungrateful ape.*

And she said *I* was stubborn. A better friend would probably have argued more. It was a risk, even though Syl had already proved that she could happily stay in cat form for months on end. But I kind of needed the moral support. Or immoral, in Syl's case.

I sighed. She was a big girl; she could make her own decisions. "We'd better get moving, then. Once Alberto discovers that Jake doesn't have the ring, the shit's really going to hit the fan."

I threw a few things in a backpack. My knives, I still wore in their sheaths; the ring was in my pocket—there wasn't much else I needed. Just my human ID, a couple of changes of clothes, and all the money I had stashed down the back of my underwear drawer. They may have hated shapers in the human territories, but they liked their money just fine. I left my phone in the bedside drawer: I'd been tracked via the phone before, and I wasn't going to fall for that again.

I took a long look around the little apartment. Closed the kitchen window that I always left open so Syl could come and go. Straightened the throw hanging over the back of the couch so that it hid the tear in the seat. I didn't want to leave this place, or the new friends I'd made here. But hopefully it wouldn't be for long. I could even give the damn ring to Alberto for safekeeping once I'd had my questions answered. He'd forgive me, then, for taking off with it. Probably.

Bag over my shoulder, I hurried out onto the landing and met Joe coming out the door of Number 1 across the hall. One eyebrow rose at sight of the backpack.

"You going somewhere? I was just coming to ask if you wanted to see the baby now she's all cleaned up." His eyes softened and a goofy smile played around his lips as he spoke of his new daughter, a smile that said *proud daddy* loud and clear. "Rosie's bringing Cody over to meet his new little sister."

"I'd love to, but I've got a train to catch." My car was still in Crosston where I'd left it last night. I'd have to catch the train in and pick it up before I could get to Newport. There was no train service connecting the shaper territories with the human ones. If I didn't want to walk the whole way, I'd have to risk showing my face again in Crosston.

"Is something wrong? Because if you need help—if you need anything—you just let me know." He closed the distance between us and took both my hands in his big ones. "After what you did for Holly, you're pack now."

If it hadn't been for me, Holly and her baby would never have been in danger in the first place. Trust Joe to forget that bit. He had a heart bigger than the great outdoors. Even Syl liked him, and cat shifters weren't usually big on werewolves. She wound round his legs now, rubbing her head affectionately against his jeans.

He reached down and picked her up. "That goes for you, too. Holly tells me there's more to you than meets the eye. I can smell it on you now." He held the cat in front of his face and gave her a little shake. Syl stared back, unblinking, her long black body dangling from his grip like a fur stole. "Why don't you come out of there and say hello properly?"

I scooped her out of his big hands and held her against my chest. "Maybe later. We've really got to get going now."

"What's the rush?"

"I need my car back. I'm going to catch the train into the city and pick it up."

He was shaking his head before I'd finished the sentence. "Crosston is the last place you should be going right now. Sounds to me like you made quite an impression there. It's not safe."

I shrugged. "I can't just abandon my car there. It could lead the provosts straight back to me." Not that it had a label saying *If found, please return to Berkley's Bay*. But it was still registered to my Crosston address, and that would give them a name to attach to the CCTV footage they no doubt had of the fight in the plaza.

"Then *I'll* head into the city tomorrow and pick it up. You can stay here where it's safe."

"But I need a car *now*, Joe. I had a call from home. My mother's sick."

"Well, why didn't you say so? Take mine."

"I couldn't do that—"

He folded his arms across his broad chest. "Not up for discussion. We can use Holly's if we need to go out. Stay right there." He disappeared into his apartment and came back carrying a set of keys, which he pressed into my hand.

"Thanks, Joe." I stood on tiptoe and kissed his bristly cheek. "I appreciate it."

"Hey, save those kisses for Lucas. I'm taken."

I punched his arm. Lucas was the brother he'd been

trying to set me up with since I'd moved in. "You know you're my favourite werewolf. How could anyone else measure up?"

Then I hurried down the stairs, still carrying Syl, before he could think of a good comeback. At the bottom, I shook my hand out. *Note to self: don't punch werewolves. They have muscles like bloody bricks.*

Joe's big diesel engine rumbled into life first go.

Syl eyed me from the passenger seat. *So now we're stealing cars from our friends too? It wasn't enough just to endanger their lives?*

Well, that was a low blow. It wasn't as if I'd *wanted* Anders to kidnap Holly.

"It's not stealing when they give you the keys."

Semantics.

I reversed out of the parking spot, feeling like I was driving a truck. Joe's four-wheel drive was a lot bigger than my little car. "Nobody's forcing you to come, you know. In fact, I wish you wouldn't. It's not safe. You could stay here and cover for me."

Stay here and explain to Hades that you've run off with that ring they're all so worked up about? No, thanks. Besides, you need me. Someone's got to stop you from charging in and doing something stupid. There was a short pause. *More stupid, that is.*

16

"Look, it's just a quick trip. In and out, ask some questions, get some answers, home again, safe and sound. With a bit of luck, no one will even miss us."

Syl's tail flicked, showing what she thought of that idea. *You know, one of the things I hate about you is your relentless optimism. Oh, and the thrill-seeking. And the fact you never take my advice. Not to mention the way you jump straight into things without thinking them through.*

We were through town already—Berkley's Bay was only a little holiday town—and the truck turned onto the road that led to the highway.

"You done enumerating my flaws?" If Syl got into one of her moods, this could be a long trip. I was sick of arguing with her. "Feel free to go into a sulk and refuse to talk to me the whole way instead."

Her tiny pink nose lifted haughtily. *I do not sulk. And you have plenty more flaws. I could fill a book, I swear.*

"Sometimes I wonder why I like you so much."

She snorted. *Your one redeeming feature is your good taste in friends.*

After that, she settled down and appeared to go to sleep. Well, it beat listening to her bitch the whole way, but I could have done with something to distract me from my thoughts. The ring ate at them; the eerie way it whispered at the edges of my mind whenever I wore it, its words just beyond my grasp. Strange. So alien—and yet familiar

17

somehow, too, like hearing a half-forgotten childhood story again as an adult.

As if my life hadn't been messed up enough already. I'd spent years hiding the fact that I could link to animals from everyone around me. And now I had some weird-ass link to a piece of jewellery too? What the hell was wrong with me?

Not to mention that the shapers' gods were real, and at least one of them would be gunning for me the minute he worked out what had happened to that weird, whispering ring. I was banking on the fact that Hades seemed quite fond of me—hopefully he wouldn't hit the smite button straight off once he figured out what I'd done. I just hoped that Jake was still out of it. That way, it might take longer for Hades to realise he didn't have the ring. Although, the way my luck was running lately, he'd probably pulled some miraculous shaper recovery and they were both hot on my heels already.

Damn shapers. I'd always known they were trouble. I should have walked straight out of my shop the minute Jake had walked into it, and never looked back. Too late now.

And what would *he* think, when he woke up in hospital and found the ring missing? Not that I cared, of course. Just because his eyes had seemed to promise something that sent a thrill right through me, it didn't mean we had any kind of connection. We'd saved each other's lives; I didn't owe him anything more. I felt kind of bad about picking his pocket while he was wounded and half out of it, that was all. But seriously, who'd be mad enough to try robbing a fireshaper when he was fully conscious?

I turned onto the highway, feeling a little safer as the big car settled into a ground-eating speed on the long, straight road. It would take Hades and Jake a little while to figure I had the ring, even if they'd already missed it. And then they'd waste time searching Berkley's Bay for me. As long as I had a couple of hours' head start, I should be fine.

And that was when the giant dog appeared in the middle of the road.

2

I slammed on the brakes. Poor Syl went flying, arse over turkey, and fetched up in the foot well, a hissing bundle of scrabbling legs and lashing tail.

What the hell are you doing? she spat, trying to clamber back onto the seat but getting thrown around again as I swerved, trying to avoid the giant dog.

And I do mean giant. The thing was bigger than a horse—bigger than the four-wheel drive, even. Its legs were like tree trunks, and it might have looked like it was planted in the road, rock-solid, but it skittered to the side like a giant damn cockroach, blocking the way past. The two wheels on that side slid off the tarmac and onto the shoulder, and the car skidded wildly, spraying gravel as I fought for control.

The car came to a shuddering halt and rocked before settling onto its springs. I revved the motor, staring out at the nightmare on the road.

It was black, so black it seemed to eat the light, and its eyes glowed red like coals. All six of them.

Syl scrambled back onto the seat and hissed, all the fur down her back standing up. *There's a dog with three heads in the road.*

"Yeah, I noticed that."

And all three of them were focused rigidly on us. Those baleful red eyes stared, unblinking. Flames danced in their depths. Trying to swerve around the monster hadn't worked so well. Maybe a game of chicken? If I drove straight at it, who would blink first?

What the actual fuck, Lexi? There's a dog with three heads in the road.

"Heard you the first time."

It's Hades, isn't it? He's found us.

I revved the engine. I had trouble imagining the urbane Alberto taking on such a monstrous form. "I'm no expert on gods, but if you're suggesting that's actually Hades, then I'd have to say no." My hands were trembling, and I clenched them tighter about the wheel. "But I'm guessing that he's figured out where Apollo's ring went."

I was pretty rusty on my Greek mythology, but I remembered something about Hades owning a three-headed dog—though he was supposed to be guarding the gates to Hell, not standing in the middle of the main road north, growling like a goddamn earthquake. But I guess if Hell's master wanted him to, he'd follow orders like a good puppy.

I put my foot down.

Lexi!

I winced as Syl's mental shriek pierced my brain, but I drove straight at the dog.

He didn't move.

Lexi!

I stomped on the brakes just before the car thudded into the beast. Syl went flailing onto the floor again, and my breath whooshed out of me as the steering wheel slammed into my chest. There was an awful crunching sound, but the dog didn't move. One of its massive heads bent to eyeball me through the windscreen. Another decided to chomp down on the car's roof.

Metal screeched and protested, and then a small patch of daylight appeared as a piece of roof tore away. I looked up just in time to catch a faceful of giant dog slobber.

"Whoa, boy! Easy there!" I pulled a knife, wincing at the pain in my chest.

A glowing red eye as big as my hand stared down at me through the hole. It would be an easy shot, but what good were knives against a thing that size? And I only had two. Even if I took out two eyes, that still left two whole heads who were then going to be mighty pissed with me. And surely Alberto wouldn't have sent his pet to kill us. He couldn't even be sure I had the ring.

"Nice doggy! Cerberus, isn't it?"

Nice doggy? Are you out of your tiny little mind?

One of the other heads had torn a hole on the other side of the car. I shuddered at the size of the teeth in those great jaws. It could rip the whole roof off and scoop us out like beans out of a tin.

The heads swooped in again to the music of crunching metal. Muscles in those massive necks strained, and the front of the car lifted off the ground. Syl wailed and clawed her way up my body.

"Ouch! For God's sake, Syl! Are you trying to choke me?" I peeled her off my neck and held her tight.

The car swung around until we were facing back the way we'd come. Cerberus let us drop, then gave us a shove. We jerked forward. I twisted around in my seat. The monster stood behind us, watching. Waiting for something.

After a moment of intense staring, one massive, clawed foot thudded into the back of the car, jolting us a little further down the road. Looked like Hades and his dog were playing a game of fetch.

"I think he's telling us to go back," I said.

Then let's do what the nice doggy wants.

Syl's slim body was trembling in my arms. I guess a giant three-headed dog would be a cat's ultimate nightmare. She wouldn't even make a mouthful for one of the monster's heads, let alone all three.

The engine was still running, and I nudged the accelerator, putting a little distance between us and the dog. He didn't follow us—not that that helped. I needed to get past him, not run in the other direction. I wasn't giving up that easily.

Cautiously, I reached out with my mind. He was an animal, after all, even if he was a supernatural one, and animals were my specialty. To my mind's sight, he blazed like a deep red fire, and I paused. That was different to the normal white light that I saw. Did I really want to dive into the head of a monster like that?

What are you waiting for? asked Syl. *You want him to take another bite out of Joe's car? Let's go.*

"Give me a minute."

How badly did I need to get to Newport? Badly enough to link with a monster and piss off a god? Although the god was probably already pissed …

Badly enough. I slid into Cerberus's mind and peeked around.

My, but the view was different from in there. Cerberus saw the world in shadows. The car in front of him was an indistinct blur of darkness containing two blazing lights. The larger one was golden, and the smaller one burned with a clean, white radiance. I guessed that was me and Syl.

How about it, buddy? You want to wander off home and forget you ever saw us?

I didn't expect an answer. Syl could communicate in words across our link, because she was a shifter, with a human mind inside her animal body. True animals had no words, but feelings and instincts could be manipulated, and I rarely had trouble communicating my wishes non-verbally. Sometimes using words helped me push my intentions across the link, even if the recipient didn't understand them. Generally, dogs were the easiest to give suggestions to, as they were genetically inclined to want to please humans.

I wasn't prepared for the growl that reverberated inside my skull. *OUT.*

I flinched, and Syl dug her claws into me. I put more force into my suggestion, pushing the giant dog away, willing it to turn its back on the two lights glowing in the shadows. I looked over my shoulder. Cerberus was shaking all three of his huge heads, as if bothered by a buzzing insect. I renewed the pressure, severing my link with Syl so I could focus all my attention on the monster.

Cerberus howled, all three massive snouts pointed at the sky. Syl scampered up my body as if I was her own personal scratching post and batted me imperiously on the cheek. I pulled her off and dumped her on the passenger seat.

"Cut it out, Syl. I'll be back in a minute. Spot back there is one tough customer."

The door stuck, the top of the frame crumpled out of shape by Cerberus's massive jaws. I shoved hard and got it open. Syl jumped down too, but she didn't follow me as I approached the monster.

He'd stopped howling, but those blood-red eyes seemed to have trouble focusing as I approached.

"Why don't you come over in the shade?" I suggested. "You must be getting pretty hot there in the sun, with all that black fur. Wouldn't you like a nice lie down?"

The heads swayed lower on their necks. He was still fighting me, and I could feel a headache building behind my eyes. I pushed deeper into his mind. It tasted of death and echoed with the memory of a thousand screams. Ugh. Not a good place to be.

EAT YOU, he threatened.

"Not now," I said. "You're too tired for that. You need to sleep."

He staggered under the weight of my suggestion, and took a reluctant step toward the side of the road. I kept up the pressure as he took another, then another. Inch by inch, I forced him off the road and onto the green of the verge.

Grass shrivelled and died under his massive paws. When he finally collapsed to the ground, a brown stain spread across the earth as every green thing he touched withered and died. His eyelids sank lower, though a slit of red still remained visible as he fought to stay awake. One of his mouths huffed out a hot breath as he sank into sleep; it was like standing in front of an open furnace. I leapt back smartly, but he didn't stir.

Once I was sure he was out of it, I hurried back to the car, linking to Syl as I went.

There you are! Her mental tone was giddy with relief. *I didn't know what happened.*

I pressed the heels of my hands against my aching eyes. A few moments without our mental connection and she lost her shit? She was the clingiest damn cat I'd ever met. It wasn't normal. "The big guy there needed my full attention. Bad doggy did *not* want to lie down."

Syl looked back doubtfully as I turned the car around. *Is bad doggy going to stay?*

I stepped on the accelerator and the car took off. Despite the damage to the bodywork, mechanically, it was still sound. I was doing well—it was the second car I'd wrecked today, and it wasn't even lunchtime yet.

"I sure hope so. My head is going to explode if I have to do that again."

Syl gazed up at the sky through the mangled holes in the roof. *Wait until Joe sees his car. Now that will be an explosion.*

❧

We bypassed Crosston. I'd had quite enough excitement for one day already. As we passed its low roofs and waving

27

trees, I wondered if anyone had managed to get Apollo's statue back onto its plinth, or if it was still blocking traffic into the Plaza of the Sun. Jake would be in all sorts of trouble over that little stunt.

When the shaper city was just a memory in the rear-view mirror I pulled into a service station to refuel and grab something to eat. My stomach had been reminding me for some time that breakfast was a long time ago.

Talk about an action-packed morning. Jake was probably still in hospital. Shapers had better healing than regular humans, but he'd taken a bullet in the shoulder, and I hadn't even had a chance to see if it had gone straight through. Plus, there was that terrible weakness brought on by the amount of metalshaping he'd had to do. It had scared the crap out of me, wondering if he was going to die before I got him back to Berkley's Bay and safety. Not that I should care. He was a shaper, and avoiding shapers had been my number one priority for so long it had become second nature. I'd certainly never kissed one before.

"You want something?" I asked Syl before I headed into the shop. Best not to think about the kissing. That was a one-off. Or at least a two-off. Anyway, it wouldn't be happening again, that was for sure. I'd be ready for him next time, if there was a next time. It might be best not to see him again. Maybe I'd stay a bit longer in Newport. That way he'd be gone back to his big, important shaper business in the city by the time I got back.

Yeah, right. He was almost as much of a lure as the damn ring. A girl could get addicted to the feel of those strong arms around her.

Just some water, Syl said, so I got a couple of bottles and a burger for myself.

She curled up and went to sleep after that, so I had nothing to do but drive and watch the rear-view mirror for any sign of a giant three-headed dog. The ring in my pocket pressed against my hip bone, and its weight lay heavy on my mind. Why could I sense it whenever I wore it, almost as if it were an animal? All my life, I'd lived with this strange ability to link to animals, but never had I felt a connection to an inanimate bloody object before. What was next? Talking to tables and chairs?

My mother had always been evasive on the subject of my father. Said he was dead and that was all that mattered; he hadn't been a good man and we were better off without him. As a child, I'd been prepared to accept that, but it just wasn't going to cut it anymore—not if my gift was about to go off the rails. I needed to know where it had come from. It certainly wasn't from her. The first step to mastering something was to understand it, right? And master it I would. I was *not* going crazy. There had to be some logical explanation.

We'd been driving through farming country, low rolling hills dotted with sheep and cows, but now the road began to rise, climbing into densely forested hills. There were no more farmhouses, or signs of humans at all, apart from the road that wound backwards and forwards up through the hills. The land fell away steeply from the side of the road and I took the corners carefully.

On the other side of the hills, the road snaked down onto a broad plain. In the distance, a river glinted in the sunlight, and on the far side of the river, a great human city thrust its towers into the sky. Newport. On this side, guarding the bridge, a small cluster of low buildings huddled behind a barbed wire-topped fence. A heavy steel gate blocked the road.

Very little traffic travelled the road. We'd passed a few trucks, but that was all. Not many people moved between shaper and human territories, though the borders had been open for nearly a hundred years. Ever since the last war, there had been an uneasy peace, and trucks hauled goods up and down the coast freely, but apart from that, people tended to stay put. Shapers and shifters were prohibited from entering human territory, and their human sympathisers were not welcome either. Nobody travelled the other direction unless they were spying for the One Worlders.

Two guards stepped out of the gate house when I was

still a long way down the road. Any car was an uncommon enough sight on this road, but one as battered as Joe's stood out like a sore thumb. They waited by the gate, guns at the ready, until I rolled to a stop.

A row of boxy concrete buildings marched away down either side of the road beyond the gate. Past them was the bridge over the river. There were no other buildings on this side of the river—no houses, no shacks, not even any piers or boats drawn up on the pebbled shore. Bare earth stretched away either side of the road, scorched clear by nervous humans who wanted to leave no cover for shifters to sneak into their city.

One guard approached as I wound down my window. The other stayed back, covering his buddy with his gun. "ID?"

I reached into the back seat for my papers, and his gaze fell on Syl, now stretching in her seat, showing her pink tongue in a jaw-cracking yawn.

"That your cat?"

No, I'm a hitchhiker she picked up, moron.

I resisted the urge to give him a smart answer. Border guards rarely had a sense of humour. "Yes."

"Vet testing's third building on the right. You'll need to stop there for clearance."

"Vet testing?" This was news to me. "She's had all her shots."

He gave me a strange look. "Security clearance. To make sure she's a hundred per cent animal." He looked over my papers, scrutinising the photo, then handed them back through the window. "What happened to your car? Looks like something took a bite out of it." He wasn't even trying to be funny. He just looked puzzled.

"Yeah. Hit some … ah … low-hanging brick work. Nearly ripped the whole roof off." I couldn't come up with a better excuse on the spur of the moment, not with alarm bells going off in my head.

What does he mean, security clearance? Syl asked. *What are they going to do?*

The guard nodded to his companion, who went back into the gate house. The gate swung open. "Straight through," the first guard said. "Stop at the third building on the right there and take your cat in. Won't take long, and then you can be on your way."

"What will they do to my cat?"

"Inject a silver pellet under her skin." He tapped the back of his neck. "Behind the neck, just under the loose skin there. She won't even notice it. Takes a couple of minutes."

I nodded, trying to keep my expression to one of polite interest. "Okay, thank you."

He stepped back, and I drove through the open gate into the compound. The road to the city beckoned. Fences

32

topped with barbed wire surrounded the compound, but no gate stood between me and the bridge, just a straight stretch of road.

What do we do? Syl asked. *Keep driving?*

There was no way we could let anyone inject her with a silver pellet. Shifters and silver just did not mix. And obviously that was the plan. I almost had to admire it. It was an ingenious way of making sure no shifters sneaked into their city in their animal forms. I bet if I hadn't had papers identifying me as a human born in Newport, I would have been getting introduced to the sharp end of an injection too.

I stopped outside the building the guard had pointed out. A glance back showed that the gate was now closed, but the guard stood beside it, watching me. Evidently he was going to make sure I did as instructed and took my terrifying cat in for testing. What would he do if I made a run for it?

The city ahead was surrounded by a high wall. There were gun emplacements on top of those walls, and soldiers patrolling. No wall was high enough to keep out a determined earthshaper, of course, but the humans did what they could to protect themselves. Those guns would certainly be enough to take out one battered four-wheel drive if I tried to bolt with Syl across the bridge.

"When I open the door, take off."

Where to? There's nowhere to hide.

True enough. The compound was military-tidy, containing nothing besides the handful of buildings and a few cars belonging to the people inside them. No vegetation, no dark alleys. Nowhere for a small black cat to lose itself.

"Run around behind the buildings. I'll run after you and distract the guard, and you can come back and hide in the car. Get under the seat."

It wasn't much of a plan, and it very much depended on my being allowed to leave with my cat supposedly still missing, but it was the best I could do. Syl obediently leapt out of the car the minute the door creaked open and bolted between two of the buildings. I jumped out after her.

"Fluffy! Come back!"

Leaving the door wide open, I hurried after her. The guard said something to his companion in the gate house then stomped down the road toward us. When I popped back out from between the buildings, he was standing there, his face drawn into a scowl, weapon up.

"Did you see where my cat went?" I asked, but I went to peer around the corner of the next building without waiting for an answer.

"You should have had that cat in a carrier." He trailed after me, his gun swinging from side to side as if he expected armed assailants to leap out from between the buildings, instead of a small black cat.

"Normally she's so good. She must have been tired of sitting after the long trip. Can you help me find her? Fluffy! Fluffy, where are you?"

He was past the car now. If I could just get him away from the road, I could call Syl back and he wouldn't see her hop into the car. He reached for the walkie talkie on his belt. "I'll get some extra personnel out here. If she won't come to you, ma'am, we'll have to destroy her."

Shit. These bastards mean business. Syl sounded close, though I couldn't see her.

Move it, Syl. With a few more people out here, Syl wouldn't stay hidden much longer. *If you can't get to the car, try the river.*

The river? I couldn't swim that. I'm a cat, not a bloody dolphin.

If you don't want to be shot, you may not have a choice. This would never have happened if you didn't insist on clinging to your damn cat form.

A sudden burst of gunfire shattered the air, and I ducked instinctively, turning my head toward the sound. But it wasn't aimed at us. The guard at the gate house had opened fire on the monster standing on the other side of the gate. Oh, shit. Cerberus had found us.

Now, Syl! We've got company.

The other guard lost all interest in the search for the missing cat. He ran toward the new threat, unloading his gun into the monster's chest. The three heads watched him come dispassionately, unaffected by his bullets. And then they swung to look at me.

STOP, the beast thundered into my mind.

Yeah, right. Stopping wasn't exactly my preferred option when a giant, three-headed dog was after me. Syl streaked past and leapt through the open car door. I hurled myself after her. The key was still in the ignition, and I turned it and slammed the car into reverse before I'd even settled in my seat.

Cerberus simply walked through the gate, bulling it out of the way with his massive chest. It creaked and strained, then burst off its hinges. It hadn't been built to withstand hell hounds. He ignored the men and their guns, all his eyes locked on me.

Tyres squealed as I took off, and Cerberus broke into a lumbering run. Away across the river, an alarm began to shrill, but I was on the bridge already. Cerberus put on a burst of speed, and so did I, revving the hell out of the engine.

Leave me alone! I shouted at him, putting all the mental force I could muster into the command. *Stop following me!*

As I roared across the bridge, I glanced in the rear-view mirror, terrified that I'd see the monster right on my tail. But he'd stopped at the river's edge and stood watching, glowing red eyes unblinking.

Really? That had worked? I could hardly believe it.

I eased off the accelerator as the car passed under the shadow of the massive archway into the city. Two groups of guards struggled with the heavy gates. They'd stood open since the last wars, so long ago that they were now frozen in place. I was glad of the diversion—I didn't want to be stopped and questioned about the frightening apparition outside the city. I made a few quick turns, losing us in the traffic.

Syl retracted her claws, releasing her death grip on the upholstery, and looked up at me. *What happened to Dog Breath?*

"He didn't cross the bridge." Had he really stopped because I'd told him to? Or was there some other reason?

Thank the gods for that. Do you think he's scared of humans?

I snorted. "I doubt he's scared of anything." Perhaps Hades had called him back just at that moment. No, that would be too much of a coincidence. "I just hope he's not going to pop up in the middle of town somewhere when we least expect it."

Maybe he can't cross running water.

"Maybe." It seemed unlikely. Why would running water bother a being who could apparently materialise out of thin air? Amazing as it seemed, he must have stopped at my command. The question was—how long would that command hold him?

My hand crept to the lump in my pocket. This ring must really be something special for Hades to send his hell hound after it. I was looking forward to getting some answers.

3

The fortifications at the bridge didn't surround the whole city—it was way too big. Beyond the river, the human lands stretched for miles.

Newport hadn't always been that big, of course. In the days of the human/shaper wars, the human settlement had huddled in on itself for protection, surrounded by walls. But in a hundred years of peace, the city had prospered and spread out, forgetting to be quite so paranoid. To the south the river still gave some protection, but to the north, the city sprawled like a drunk. There was only one shaper city to the north, a day's drive away. Out of sight, out of mind.

Newport's fortunes seemed to be looking up—as we made our way through the snarls of traffic, the sounds of pneumatic drills echoed through the canyons between the skyscrapers. The skyline was dotted with cranes. Practically every block had some kind of new construction going up, as if Newport's rich uncle had died and now she was spending all his money tarting herself up.

As I drove further from the bridge and the heart of the city, the streets took on a more familiar grime. Crime and poverty were both way more common in Newport than in the shaper cities. Some people figured that was a small price to pay to be out from under the shaper yoke. Others were simply too afraid to consider that there might be a better life somewhere else. We passed boarded-up shops and crumbling old apartment buildings. A skinny dog with patchy-looking fur rooted through garbage on the side of the road. Passers-by ignored it. A lot of them were skinny too.

How far to your mother's house? Syl asked.

"Half an hour or so."

Do you think she'll be pleased to see you?

Probably not, since last time I saw her she'd been kicking me out of home. *This is all your fault!* she'd screamed. The men had just carried my brother's body away, his bright hair matted with blood. *Get out.*

They accused me of being a shaper? Fine. I'd go to the shaper city, then, and see what welcome I got there. Better than I had in my own hometown, as it turned out. Syl had taken me in after one chance meeting, and her circle of friends had virtually adopted me. Shifters tended to prefer the company of their own kind, but Syl usually got what she wanted. I hadn't told anyone but Syl what I could do, however. The habit of keeping quiet about my abilities was well-established by then, and I saw no reason to draw attention to myself. I knew I was no shaper, whatever the humans thought, and seeing them in action didn't make me want to get to know them any better. They were arrogant and inconsiderate. As I had found out all too soon, they could also be murderous.

"My mother's not the forgiving type. I haven't heard from her since I left."

I hadn't called her either, but then, I hadn't been the one doing the throwing out. I figured it was up to her to make the first move, if there was ever to be a reconciliation. Not that I was holding my breath for that. Her "get out" had sounded pretty final.

What makes you think she'll talk to you now, then?

"This time, I'm not giving her a choice." I'd camp out on her front lawn if I had to, but I wasn't leaving until I had some answers.

The apartment buildings gave way to tiny terrace houses, all stacked up in rows against each other, and then, as we got further into the suburbs, individual houses on small blocks began to appear. None of them were as large or attractive as most of the houses even in Berkley's Bay, though here, too, I noticed some new construction. Money was tight in the human territories, but apparently some people had cash to spare. For most, even if you were lucky enough to have a job, you were only paid enough to scrape a bare living. Mining was where the big money was, but if you wanted to live in the city, options were scarcer. Lawyers and bankers always prospered, of course, but the working classes couldn't afford that kind of education.

My mother had a freestanding house in one of the outer suburbs. I pulled up across the street from it and cut the engine.

We're here? Syl peered out the window with interest.

My childhood home was much as I remembered it. The small, red-brick house had been built not long after the end of the wars, and it was showing its age in the sagging gutters and cracks in the façade. But it would probably still be here in another hundred years even so. The front door was white, now, instead of the blue I remembered, and some of the bushes out front had got taller, but mostly, it looked just the same.

I took a deep breath and got out of the car. No one else was on the street. It was only mid-afternoon—too early for the workers to be home yet. Mum had a part-time cleaning job; she might be home or not. I didn't know her schedule.

The blinds were drawn on the front window, so I couldn't peer in. I knocked and waited a few moments, but no one came to the door.

You got a key? Syl asked.

"No." I'd run out with only the clothes I was standing in, my wallet and phone in my pockets. I hadn't even stopped for a toothbrush. My whole life had been left behind in my rush to escape my mother's screaming hate. I'd hitched a ride with a trucker heading south and made my way to Crosston with no idea what to do with myself or a cent to my name.

I let myself through the side gate into the tiny, paved courtyard out the back. My old bedroom was back here, and the lock on the window had always been dodgy. I jiggled the window back and forth until the tongue popped free, then I climbed in, shutting the window behind me.

I landed on the same old blue patterned carpet, but everything else about the room was different. Gone was my bed and sturdy wardrobe. Now the room was set up as a sitting room. Ratty old cane chairs with faded floral cushions clustered around a small cane table, positioned to get the afternoon sun through the big windows. Guess Mum hadn't wasted any time removing all traces of her despised daughter. She'd torn down all my posters and repainted the walls a cheery yellow. There was no sign, now, that this had once been a teenaged girl's bedroom.

Well, what had I expected? That she would have seen the error of her ways and left it as a shrine to her lost daughter? She knew my phone number. She could have called me any time in the last year if she'd wanted to make peace. No point feeling hurt at the speed with which she'd discarded me.

On a table by one of the cane chairs sat a large framed photo. Two smiling faces beamed into the camera. One was a good-looking guy about my own age; the other was a middle-aged woman. Probably his mother, judging by how similar those smiles were. I'd never seen either of them before.

I opened the door and stepped out into the hallway, Syl at my heels. The house was quiet but for the ticking of the grandfather clock in the cramped foyer. That clock was a legacy from her own parents, and way too big for the space in which it now found itself, but she would never hear of getting rid of *that*. It was only daughters that were easily disposable.

A row of photos hung on the wall. Most featured the same guy from the big photo I'd just seen—some younger, some older. There were even a couple featuring a curly-headed youngster who was probably a younger incarnation of the same mystery guy. Why my mother had him plastered all over her house, I couldn't imagine. Where were all the photos of my brother and me that used to hang here? Even if those memories were too painful to keep, why replace them with a stranger?

We wandered into the kitchen, where Syl leapt up onto the benchtop and sniffed around for food. *Do you reckon *your mother's got any tins of tuna hidden around here?** she asked.

I went straight to the right cupboard. Everything here was exactly as I remembered it: the worn benches, the sink polished to a shine, the ugly brown linoleum still peeling in the corner by the back door. The kitchen was almost as cramped as the one back in my tiny apartment in Berkley's Bay, with a round table and four wooden chairs taking up all the remaining floor space.

I set the open tin of fish on the floor for Syl, then whirled at a voice behind me.

"Who the hell are you? And what are you doing in my kitchen?"

The middle-aged woman from the photo stood there, a fearful expression on her face. She was about my mother's age, but definitely wasn't my mother. Who the hell was I? Who the hell was *she*?

"I'm Lexi," I said. "Rita's daughter."

"Rita who?"

"Jardine. The woman who owns this house."

"Girl, I've lived in this house going on twenty years, and I don't know any Rita. She certainly doesn't own it." She stepped back warily. "If you're looking for money, I don't keep any in the house. Get out or I'll call the police."

I held up my open hands, palms facing her. "Lady, I'm not here to rob you. I'm just here to see my mother. And no offence, but you haven't lived here for twenty years. I grew up in this house."

The woman must have dementia, though she seemed young for it. Or maybe she'd just moved in. But that couldn't be right. All my mother's stuff was still here. I recognised everything except for the photos. This woman couldn't be living here.

She backed away, pulling a phone out of her pocket. "I'm calling the police right now. You have three seconds to get out of my house."

The phone shook, giving the lie to her calm tone, but she didn't take her eyes off me as she dialled. I backed away too, towards the back door, my head spinning. I just couldn't make sense of it. Why was she pretending this was her house? But what were all those photos doing here? Where were the ones of my brother and me that used to hang in the hall?

I felt behind me for the doorknob. It fitted into my hand like an old friend, familiar and comfortable. My hand had helped to wear that smoothness into it over the years, from the time I was tall enough to reach it until the day I left home. Anger and frustration warred within me. Why was this woman lying to me?

But there was no use waiting around to argue the point with the police. They might remember me and my family, even if this woman didn't. I turned the knob. The door still stuck a little on the frame as I yanked it open, just as it always had. "It's all right. I'm going."

I stepped outside and Syl followed me. As soon as I was down the steps, the woman hurried over and closed the door behind us. The click of the lock engaging made me want to hurl myself at the door and demand answers. With some effort, I controlled myself and stomped back down the side passage and through the gate into the front yard.

Where was my mother, and why had this woman stolen her life? And what the hell could I do about it?

Guess we won't be bunking down at your mum's tonight, Syl said as she settled herself into the front seat. *Who was that woman?*

I let my head fall forward against the steering wheel and took a deep breath, trying to get control of myself. I was shaking from fury and shock. Where to now? What had happened to my mother?

"Never seen her before." I started the car and pulled out abruptly. There was a dingy old motel a few blocks away where I could get a room. If it was still there. If I wasn't going completely mad.

We turned a corner and drove past my old school, the playground scuffed to dirt by the passage of many little feet. Of course the damn motel would be there. The landscape of my childhood was unchanged, every building recognisable. There was the post office, and there, the pawn shop, its front window caged behind steel bars. There was the row of identical little box houses built nearly a century ago, when the government had had notions of building the city up again after the war.

Had the government taken my mother away? Or the One Worlders? But why? And why would they plant some strange woman in her place? Surely not in an effort to get their hands on me. That seemed like a hell of a lot of trouble to go to. They didn't know where I'd gone, or if I'd ever return. And why should they care, anyway? I was nobody special.

I took a room and paid for a single night, not sure how long I'd be staying. The motel had a "no pets" policy, so I shoved Syl under my jacket and sneaked her up the stairs. The concrete steps were scabrous and the stairwell stank of urine. When I unlocked my door, it was a pleasant surprise to find the room clean, if a little shabby.

Syl hopped up onto the bed and I threw myself down beside her. The ceiling had a water stain near the door that led into the tiny bathroom. The light fitting was a bare globe suspended from a short cord. The little room looked weird from this angle, though it was kind of fitting, considering how my whole damn world had just been turned upside down. I put my hands behind my head and sighed.

"I don't know what to do." Finding a stranger apparently in possession of my mother's house had completely thrown me. We hadn't ever been close, but she was still my mother. If something bad had happened to her—if she needed my help and I'd been sulking in the shaper territories, waiting for her to call—my gut wrenched at the thought. "Where do I even begin looking now?"

Syl climbed onto my chest and glared down at me. *Who's the one with the special gift for finding things, hmm?*

I groaned. "Come off it, Syl, have you seen the size of this place? It could take months to search the whole thing."

Then it will take months. In which case, I suggest you get started. The sooner we get out of here and back to shaper territory, the happier I'll be.

"I told you not to come." My irritation with her threatened to swell into outright anger. "You could have been home safe in Berkley's Bay. Joe and Holly would have looked after you."

God, I wished I was there now. Panic fluttered in my stomach. I felt so helpless—what could I *do*?

Impatiently, I pushed Syl off, and she curled up next to my neck, her fur warm and tickly on my skin. *Pity we didn't bring that hunky fireshaper along. He might have had a few ideas, and he was pretty handy in a fight.*

"Let's hope there'll be no fighting." I was *not* going to think about Jake now; I had enough on my plate. Kissing someone a couple of times didn't constitute a relationship, however tempting the idea of taking it further might have been. True, it had felt good to have him at my back, but that didn't mean I trusted him. I wasn't stupid. And he sure wouldn't trust *me* any more, considering I'd taken off with his precious ring. That thought hurt more than I wanted to admit.

I pulled the ring from my pocket and stared at its spiralling sunrays. This thing sure had caused a lot of trouble for something so small.

It's pretty, Syl said. *A little over the top for my taste, but pretty.*

It *was* kind of flamboyant. I turned the ring from side to side, watching the golden rays catch the light from the dim bulb overhead. "Anders told me it was the 'avatar of Apollo'. Do you have any idea what that means?"

Nope. You should have asked your mate Hades.

"It didn't seem like a good idea to bring it up. He seemed awfully keen to get his hands on it." I slipped the ring onto the middle finger of my right hand. The sunrays extended over the fingers on each side. As it settled into place, I again had that sensation of hearing voices, indistinct, as if from the next room. Was it trying to talk to me? If only I could understand it. But how could a piece of jewellery communicate with me? That was a crazy way to think. When I was contemplating a chat with a hunk of inanimate metal, it was clearly time to get more sleep.

"I think I need an early night. We can start searching tomorrow."

Nuh-uh. Syl waggled her head at me in a very uncatlike way. *That three-headed monstrosity could turn up on our doorstep any time. You need to go back there tonight and check that house from top to bottom, see if you can find any leads on what happened to your mum.*

I sighed. I was stuffed, and the ring's faint whisperings on the edge of my mind set my teeth on edge, but she was right. For all I knew, that woman had my mother imprisoned in her own house. I had to check it out.

"Fine. I'll sleep and you can wake me up around midnight."

The ring was going to be a problem. It was too valuable to leave in a motel room. I didn't want to wear it, but I was afraid it might fall out of my pocket. Whatever it was or wasn't, losing it seemed like a bad idea.

"Pity this thing's so distinctive. I don't want to be memorable." If I was going to be sneaking around the city in search of my mother, the last thing I wanted was for anyone to notice me and wonder what I was up to. I'd had my fill of police attention in this neighbourhood; I needed to slip under the radar entirely.

The whispering got louder, until I could almost make out words, except they didn't seem to be in any language I recognised. And then the ring writhed on my finger like a live thing. I clapped my other hand over my mouth to muffle my startled squeak.

Syl leapt up, spooked. *What's wrong?*

"The ring!"

I held my hand out to her, and it was shaking. The ring that circled my middle finger was now a plain gold band. Had I done that, or had it?

4

I parked around the corner from the house, down beside the school. It was past midnight and there were no lights showing in the windows of the houses across the road. Half the streetlights were out too. Maintenance wasn't a high priority in the human territories. There was never enough money for all the things that needed doing. I'd been spoiled in Berkley's Bay, with all the modern conveniences on tap. I remembered blackouts that went on for days during my childhood. Petrol shortages, too, and even the occasional time when the supermarket's shelves stood half empty, and the frown on my mother's face never seemed to go away.

The shaper territories had it easy compared to the human ones. It was just a shame about the bloody shapers. Shifters I had no issue with, but shapers were another matter entirely. Anders had soured me forever on the arrogant bastards. I'd never met a shaper yet who wouldn't be improved by a long trip off a short pier. Not even Jake—though I might save him from drowning after his pride had been dunked sufficiently. Heck, I'd be happy to offer him mouth-to-mouth.

I grinned at the memory of our last mouth-to-mouth encounter. Whatever I thought of his arrogance and his habit of getting what he wanted with threats, I had to admit the man could kiss.

I brushed my fingers across my lips and the grin faded as I felt the ring on my finger. I was pretty sure I hadn't suddenly acquired some mystical ring-altering power, which meant the ring had changed itself. Did that mean it had heard my wish and granted it? Was the damn thing *eavesdropping* on me? Maybe I should wish to win the lottery while I was at it. I shivered, though the night was warm for spring. The whole thing was creepy, and I was scared and out of my depth.

Syl slinked along behind me, invisible in the shadows. As always, she'd refused my advice to stay safely in our motel room. For someone who was such a scaredy cat, she courted danger surprisingly often. Seemed like her biggest fear was being left alone in this hostile city. She was prepared to take her chances with a bit of breaking and entering.

Not that that should be an issue. No one saw us ghost down the dark street and around the corner. Mum's house was about halfway down. Like its neighbours, it was completely dark. Its inhabitant, whoever she was, had most likely been asleep a couple of hours by now. I stifled a yawn. I could do with a bit of shut-eye myself, but my need to know what the hell was going on wouldn't let me sleep. Was my mother asleep in there, too, a prisoner in her own house?

You stay here, I told Syl when we were opposite the house. *Keep an eye out and let me know if anyone comes.*

Sure thing. She slipped under a bush in someone's front yard and disappeared.

I crossed the street, my sneakers noiseless on the cracked road surface. My eyesight, boosted by my connection to Syl, adjusted to the dark and I slipped quietly down the side of the house. The gate creaked ever so slightly as I opened it, but there was no one but me to hear. I picked my way across the lawn to the same window I'd gone through earlier in the day. A little judicious jiggling and the lock again popped free, and I climbed into my remodelled bedroom as quietly as I could. This time, I didn't close the window behind me, in case I needed a quick exit.

I'd brought a tiny flashlight with me, but I didn't want to risk its light until I'd checked the woman's whereabouts. The house was still; the only noise was the ticking of the big grandfather clock in the hall, so she probably wasn't sitting up watching late-night television, but it paid to be cautious. For all I knew she was an insomniac knitter, ready to spear me with a knitting needle if I started waving my light around.

Easing the door open soundlessly, I stepped into the hall—where powerful hands grabbed me and slammed me into the wall. Adrenaline flooded my body at the unexpectedness of it. For a split second, I couldn't move, my head throbbing from where it had smashed against the wall, then I dropped the flashlight and kicked out furiously. A couple of kicks connected, and my attacker grunted in pain, but he had my arms pinned. I writhed in panic, but I couldn't get free.

I copped a blow to the head that set my ears ringing, and I gave up the struggle, sagging against the wall like a sack of potatoes. There was a muffled curse as the unexpected weight caught him by surprise, then he flicked on the hall light.

Blinking in the sudden brightness, I found myself facing the man from all the photos. His face still smiled out at me from the frames opposite, but the real man wasn't smiling. His brows were drawn together into a furious glare. He wasn't much taller than me, but solidly built—his strength evident in the way he kept me pinned with only one arm while the other drew a gun.

"Now, then," he said, stepping back to cover me with the weapon. "Who are you and what are you doing in my mother's house?"

"*Your* mother's?" I returned his glare with interest. My upper arms would be bruised tomorrow from the force of his grip. "Who the hell are you people? What have you done with my mother?"

"Adrian? I heard noises. What's going on?" The woman from earlier came out of her room, pulling on a dressing gown. Actually, scratch that. She came out of my mother's room. I caught a glimpse of Mum's familiar quilt on the bed before she closed the door. She stopped short when she saw me.

"I'd say your visitor is back, Mum. Unless there's more than one deranged female claiming you stole her mother's house."

"Yes, that's her." His mother's face was flinty. Guess she didn't like being woken up in the middle of the night. "What does she want?"

Lexi? What's happening? Syl asked. *I see a light in there.*

There was a welcoming party waiting for me. Stay put. I'll call you if I need you.

Syl wouldn't be any use against a gun, and I wasn't going to risk her.

"That's what I plan to find out." Adrian jerked the gun toward the kitchen. "This way."

Obediently, I moved down the hall. Adrian's mother followed him, whispering furiously. My augmented hearing caught every frantic word. "It's because of these Shadowers, isn't it? I told you not to get involved with them! I'm ringing the police."

"Mum!" His head turned ever so slightly toward her, and I took my chance.

Two leaping steps took me to the grandfather clock looming over the hallway. I heaved at the top of the case and sent it crashing down in their path, narrowly missing Adrian's head. The gun boomed, but the massive clock took the bullet.

I sprinted for the back door with Syl yelling frantically into my head about gunshots.

I'm okay! I yelled back. *A little busy right now!*

Adrian scrambled over the ruins of the clock and came after me. As his mother screeched in the hallway, I wrenched the door open, my shoulders tensed in expectation of a bullet. None came, and I leapt from the doorway to the ground, bypassing the steps completely.

Adrian followed me over the handrail, but his landing wasn't as sure as mine. Here in the dark, I had all the advantages. My sight and agility were already sharpened by my link to Syl. As I ran, I cast my mind out for other allies.

There wasn't much to work with. They weren't big on pet animals in the human territories, due to their fear of shifters. In a shaper city this size, there'd be fifty or more cats in the immediate vicinity. Here I found only two, and they were both locked inside. Probably their owners were afraid of what their neighbours might do to them if they caught them outside in the dark. There were more dogs, since there were no dog shifters, but dogs weren't a lot of use, trapped inside their own backyards.

I ran for the side gate, but the latch chose that moment to stick. Instead of wasting time with it, I vaulted over the side fence into the neighbour's yard. Maybe it would be better to run through a few backyards instead of heading for the open street. With my agility, the fences would prove little obstacle, but they might slow down my pursuer. There was also more cover if he decided to get trigger happy again.

Lights flicked on in the neighbour's house as I sprinted across their backyard, no doubt because of the gunshot. A dog three yards over had started barking the minute the gun went off, and he hadn't let up yet. A nice, deep bark that promised a sizeable animal. That, I could work with.

I was almost across the yard when Adrian topped the fence. He balanced there for a second, lit by the light streaming from his neighbour's back windows. He wasn't holding the gun any more, but his expression as his eyes met mine wasn't pleasant. Perhaps he hadn't found the episode with the grandfather clock quite as satisfying as I had. I'd always hated that clock, keeping me awake at night with its stupid bonging. Why should he care that it was kindling all over the hallway now? It wasn't even his.

Using a conveniently placed garbage bin, I bounded to the top of the fence in front of me and landed lightly on the other side in three giant steps. There were no lights on in this house. Perhaps they were heavy sleepers, or maybe no one lived there. The grass was tall and unkempt, as if it were a long time since it had seen the business end of a lawn mower. I sprinted straight across to the next fence, my steps sure in the dark.

I found an owl and called her to me. She was hunting rodents in a small patch of bushland that meandered along the backs of houses a few streets over, following the course of a small stream. That was a piece of luck. She was a big one, too, with long vicious claws. She'd make Adrian wish he'd taken his chances with the grandfather clock.

A metallic clanging behind me announced that he'd found the same garbage bin I'd just used, but he hadn't been quite so successful at using it as a springboard. A string of curses rent the night, bringing a grin to my face and provoking a renewed flurry of barking from my deep-voiced friend.

The next fence was taller than the previous ones. When I hauled myself to the top, I found a mass of prickly bushes waiting on the other side. Like a tightrope walker, I ran lightly along the narrow top of the fence until I found a safer place to leap down. I was across that yard and astride the next fence before there was any sign of my pursuer.

Perhaps it would be safe, soon, to head for the street, where I could make better time.

From the top of the fence, I looked down at the dog. He was a huge black thing that blended with the night. Dark eyes, black nose, with a short coat and pointed ears—the only part of him that showed plainly in the dim light was his teeth. My mental touch had calmed his barking, and his stump of a tail thrashed a welcome against the grass as he gazed up at me rapturously, tongue lolling from his open mouth. If he'd been trained as a guard dog, he might have been useful, but he wasn't looking particularly terrifying at the moment. Getting him to attack anyone might prove impossible. He was all bark.

But you never knew. With a bit of luck, Adrian might have been terrified of dogs since he was a kid. I hurried across the yard. I could hear him coming. He was certainly persistent.

Will you quit messing around and get your arse back to the car? Syl demanded. *What are you doing back there?*

Just setting up a welcome of my own. I'll be there soon. You could always bring the car around if you're worried, and save me having to flee down the road from a gun-wielding maniac. I couldn't resist the urge to twist the knife just a little. Syl had to get over this fear of taking her human form.

A gun-wielding—! You said you were fine!

I am. Relax. The owl would be here any moment.

61

Between her and the dog, I could keep Adrian occupied nicely. But as far as information-gathering efforts went, the night had been a bust. I still knew nothing about these people who'd taken over my mother's life as well as her house.

One of these days, you're going to give me a heart attack.

Admit it. You were bored before you met me. Adrian's head appeared above the fence line. At my signal, the dog threw himself against the fence with great enthusiasm, barking up a storm. *Gotta go. Be with you in a minute.*

To my surprise, the man leapt down into the yard with no sign of fear and laid a hand on the dog's head. "Easy, boy."

The traitorous dog sat at his feet and commenced the same tail-wagging routine he'd performed for me. Figured. Of course—if Adrian lived just down the street, he probably knew the dog well. I leapt to the top of the next fence. I could still set the animal on him if I pushed it hard enough. If I could put Cerberus to sleep, hell, I could make this dog rip his throat out if I wanted to.

"Stop," Adrian said. "I'm not going to hurt you. Who are you?"

I glared down at him. My arms hurt and my head still throbbed from when he'd slammed me against the wall. "You probably shouldn't go around firing guns at people if you don't mean to hurt them."

"That was an accident. The gun went off when you nearly flattened me with that damn clock." He made no move to approach, just stood there with his hand on the dog's head. The dog nudged the hand impatiently with his nose, obviously not happy with the lack of attention, and Adrian absently scratched behind its ears. "Not that I'm not grateful for the destruction of that hideous clock, but you scared the hell out of my mother, showing up this afternoon and telling her it wasn't her house. I can't let you just run off after something like that."

Well, damn. I'd almost started liking him for the clock comment, but if he thought he could tell me what I could and couldn't do, we weren't going to be friends.

"Try and stop me," I said, and leapt down the other side of the fence.

I sprinted across the yard, hearing the sound of pursuit accompanied by some enthusiastic barking from the dog. What had happened to my owl? I cast my mind out and found her, way off course. While I'd been distracted, she'd slipped from my control and disappeared about her own business. Firmly, I guided her in the direction I wanted.

I glanced back and saw Adrian straddling the fence behind, but he made no move to jump down and chase me. Instead he raised his hands as if he were a shaper, and made a beckoning movement.

Surely there were no shapers here, living among the humans? What was he doing?

Ouch! I slapped a hand to my neck, where something had just bitten me. I drew my hand away and found a dead bee in my palm. Not bitten, then—stung. What the hell? Bees weren't nocturnal. And then I heard an ominous noise—the soft hum of a swarm on the move.

A dark, amorphous shape moved between me and the soft light of the moon, and the buzzing grew louder. Incredulous, I glanced at Adrian, who still held his arms aloft, an expression of concentration on his face. Was he controlling these bees?

A few outliers reached me and tried to sting. Now that I was aware of them, I ordered them away with a thought. I flicked a couple at Adrian, and saw him flinch as they stung him. The rest of the swarm headed my way, bent on their mission.

This was incredible. He really was controlling them, but how? No shaper I'd ever heard of could have done a thing like that. They only worked with the elements, not creatures. I raised my own arms in mockery of his pose. However he was doing it, he was about to discover that two could play at that game.

The swarm changed direction mid-flight. I sent them hurtling toward him, their angry buzzing full of menace. The dog, at least, had the good sense to run away, but the man stood his ground.

"You're an Aristaean too?" he shouted above the bees' noise. He waved his arms furiously, and the swarm rotated around him like a slow-moving tornado, close but not touching. "Why didn't you say so? Don't go!"

His arm-waving finally had an effect, though the strain showed on his face. The living tornado began to break up, bees swirling off harmlessly into the darkness as I froze. What the hell was an Aristaean? Were he and I the same, then? All this time, I'd thought I was the only one. Always fearful, hiding my odd ability. Were there other people just like me? My heart leapt at the thought.

I stared at him across the dark backyard, transfixed. Maybe I wasn't some weird anomaly after all. I stared as if I could see into his soul, and he returned my gaze, as still as a man trying not to spook a nervous horse. The moment stretched out, hope soaring as high as the owl above.

And then I heard the wail of the first siren, soon joined by another, approaching from different directions. His mother must have made good on her threat to call the police. I broke away from his gaze with reluctance. I wasn't hanging around to renew my acquaintance with the local constabulary. Time to go.

My owl was wheeling overhead, invisible in the dark. I called her down, and she plummeted out of the night sky, claws extended. Adrian screamed as her claws found him. He cowered away from her buffeting wings, arms raised protectively above his head. Taking advantage of his distraction, I slipped around the side of the house and gained the street, then set off at a steady jog to find Syl. She was never going to believe this.

5

If I'd had my phone with me I would have been hunting the internet for any mention of Aristaeans. Since I didn't, I was reduced to tossing and turning, my mind refusing to still. Were there *more* people like me in the world? Maybe a whole race of them? Or was "Aristaean" more of a job description? Either way, I couldn't sleep for the possibilities.

About three o'clock in the morning, Syl heaved a long-suffering sigh and moved from the bed next to me to the room's lone armchair. *It's like trying to sleep in a bloody tumble dryer,* she grumbled, giving me a baleful look with her green eyes. *If you can't sleep, you could at least lie still like a normal person.*

I snorted. What did I know about being a normal person? Stuff all, that's what. And now I'd been presented with the possibility that I wasn't alone in my abnormality—how could I be expected to sleep?

Eventually I did, of course, dropping off some time in the wee small hours, and waking, heavy with exhaustion, to the sound of some lunatic revving his engine in the carpark below my room.

Thank God you're awake, Syl said, stalking up my body to stand on my chest. She glared down at me, whiskers quivering. *A person could starve to death around here.*

I glanced around and found the small bedside clock. "*It's only eight o'clock.*"

Starve to death, she insisted.

"Fine." I shoved her out of the way and levered myself into an upright position. My head throbbed and my eyes were gritty from lack of sleep. Coffee was an urgent priority. "I'll head out and grab some breakfast. You stay here. I'll bring something back for you."

Tuna, she said. *And not that awful greasy stuff either. In brine.*

I rolled my eyes as I pulled yesterday's clothes back on, a little worse for wear after scrambling over fences in the middle of the night. "Yes, Master. You might have to take what you can get. They don't have the same range of luxuries in the human territories that you shifters are used to."

I left the battered truck and headed out on foot. The main shopping street was only a couple of blocks over from the motel. Maybe the walk would help clear my head. It was a cool, crisp morning, the kind of spring day that does its damnedest to hang onto winter. I missed the tang of salt on the breeze; I'd grown so used to its ever-present scent in Berkley's Bay.

I walked the familiar streets, still half-thinking of Berkley's Bay and the friends I'd left behind. How was it possible to feel homesick for a place I'd only lived three months, when I'd never missed this city I'd grown up in? I knew this place so well, my feet took me towards Belmonte's Café without my even meaning it. I'd gone there so often as a teenager, to hang out with friends, and later to work there in the afternoons after school. And yet I hadn't spared the place a thought the whole time I'd been gone.

I passed my old high school, sprawled on its block among the gum trees. Only there were a lot fewer gums now, due to the enormous new building that had risen in the middle of the old playground. That hadn't been there last time I'd passed this way. The old portable classrooms that we'd sweltered through the hot summers in had disappeared, to make way for this gleaming edifice of steel and glass. Things were looking up for Blackdale High.

Around the next corner, where a row of old terrace houses had once slumped wearily, another new building appeared. This one was a shopping village, complete with a three-storey carpark. Where was the money for these new buildings coming from?

I was tempted to go in and have a look, but I decided on Belmonte's instead, and continued on to the main street. Maybe Cath would still be working there, and if not, surely her dad would be in the kitchen, coming out to greet his regulars in his big, booming voice. Cath had been my best friend in high school. If anyone knew where my mum had ended up, it would be her.

The bell on the door tinkled as I entered Belmonte's, and the rich aroma of coffee greeted me. There was the usual hubbub of conversation, though the place was only half full at this time of day. Most people only stopped in to grab a coffee to go in the mornings; it wasn't until lunchtime that the place really got busy. Then you'd be lucky to find a seat. Harry Belmonte's pasta was a local legend.

I took a seat and ran my eye down the familiar menu. Well, some things didn't change, at least. I could practically recite it from my days of working here.

A young waitress who looked like she should still be in school hurried over, her once-black apron faded to a dull grey, the red Belmonte's logo a splash of dirty brown, the colour of dried blood. "What can I get you?" she asked, pencil poised over her pad.

I couldn't help glancing over her shoulder towards the kitchen door. Harry always liked his wait-staff to start with a cheery hello and a bit of chit-chat. He was a man who liked a chat himself, but he'd always said that customers who were treated like people rather than numbers were happy customers, and happy customers tipped better and kept coming back. Which made both Harry and the wait-staff happy too.

"I'll have the omelette with bacon and mushroom, and a flat white, thanks."

She wrote it down and headed for the kitchen without another word. She must be new. I craned to see past her as she opened the kitchen door, but I couldn't see Harry. Cath wasn't here either. She'd usually be working the coffee machine, but a young guy with a goatee was making the coffees.

The coffee came quickly and it was just as good as I remembered.

"Does Cath still work here?" I asked the waitress before she could escape again.

"Cath who?"

"Cath Belmonte. Harry's daughter."

She shook her head. "I don't know her."

Well, maybe she'd finally married that Dylan idiot and changed her name. "But Harry's here, right?"

She gave me a blank look.

"Harry Belmonte? The owner?"

The look turned from blank to odd. "The owner is Deirdre Mayer."

Funny. I never would have picked Harry as the type to give up the café. He'd been a fixture here as long as I could remember.

"Really? Harry sold out? When did that happen?"

She shrugged, already turning away, bored with the conversation. "I don't know. I've only worked here a couple of years. Deirdre's been the boss since I started."

I stared after her, my mouth gaping open. It was happening again. Deirdre had been the boss for two years? That was crap. I'd been working here myself eighteen months ago, and Harry had been in charge then. And I'd certainly never met this waitress before. But why would she lie to me?

I took a gulp of coffee and it scalded my throat all the way down. What was going on? I felt sick. It was like my whole life was being erased. I looked around the familiar room, at the cheery red-checked tablecloths, and the paintings on the walls. Everything looked exactly as it always had, but there wasn't a single person here I recognised. That didn't mean anything, of course. Newport was a big place, and even in this little corner of it, I didn't know everyone—but that didn't stop the knot in my stomach from twisting a little tighter. I rubbed my thumb back and forth across the ring on my finger, its faint whispering a constant background noise. Life was getting stranger and stranger.

My omelette came and I ate it mechanically, without tasting it. What now? A wild desire to run all over town in search of anyone I knew came over me. Surely somewhere I would find someone I recognised. I wasn't crazy—I had a lifetime of memories of this place and the people who lived here.

After choking down the last few mouthfuls, I paid the bill and left. The Belmontes had lived opposite the school. I'd always been envious of Cath for that—she could stay home in the morning until the very last minute, watching cartoons on TV. Often, she'd be running in the school gates as the bell went, her laces untied and cramming the last of her breakfast in her mouth.

If Cath *had* married Dylan the Dirt Bag, she wouldn't live there any more, but Harry obviously wasn't working at Belmonte's now, so he or Mrs Belmonte should be home. I was anxious to see a familiar face. As I passed the other shops in the row, I peeked in at each one. No Mrs G at the florist. No Chans at the counter of the dry-cleaning place, though it was still called Chan's Dry-cleaning Specialists. I began to regret the omelette, as nausea churned in my stomach. *Relax, you idiot. The Belmontes will explain everything.* But my stomach wouldn't listen.

I paused on the street outside the Belmonte house. Like my mother's house, everything still looked the same. Mrs Belmonte was a great gardener, and her garden beds were as neat and pretty as ever, full of flowers that scented the air. Bees buzzed in the sunshine, and a flight of rosellas screeched overhead as I stood, hesitating, on the footpath.

Well, this was never going to get me any answers. I pushed open the wrought-iron gate and strode up the path between the flowers.

I knocked on the glass panel beside the screen door and waited. Sounds of movement inside the house told me someone was home, but they took a long time getting to the door. Finally, it opened to reveal a tiny, white-haired man leaning heavily on a walking frame.

He squinted up at me. "Yes? Can I help you?"

This was not Harry Belmonte. Or anyone I had ever seen before in my life. I took a deep breath and tried to hold it together.

"I'm looking for the Belmontes. Do they still live here?"

"Belmontes?" He shook his head. "Never heard of them. You sure you've got the right house?"

I wasn't sure of anything any more, but this house was almost as familiar as my own. I'd spent half my damn adolescence here with Cath. "Yes. They used to live here. Do you know where they've gone? Did they leave a forwarding address?"

The head-shaking grew more pronounced, until I worried about his balance. He gave me a suspicious look. "If they used to live here, it must have been a long time ago.

As I said, I've never heard of them, and I've been here for years."

Still shaking his head, he closed the door, leaving me panting on the doorstep as if I'd just run the four-minute mile. I drew a deep, shuddering breath, trying to calm down. Losing my shit was not going to help. There had to be an explanation for this. *Had* to be. I just had to find it.

I walked back down the garden path. *The same damned path I'd walked down a thousand times before.* But there was no use thinking about that. It would drive me completely around the twist.

What else could I do? How was I going to crack this puzzle? I thought for a minute, then set off for a house around the corner. Another school friend, Charmaine Thomas. Well, "friend" might be a little generous, but she had three younger sisters, all of whom would still be at school. There was no way her family would have moved away.

No one answered my knocking. I walked around the house, peering in the windows, trying to see if it looked like a house with four daughters living in it. On the way out, I checked the letterbox. The only letter inside was addressed to a Mr Thorndike.

I swallowed hard, staring down at the letter. A feeling of panic bubbled up from deep inside. Where was everyone? Where was my history? What had happened to my life?

I went a bit crazy then, running all over the neighbourhood, knocking on every door I could remember. It was the same story at every one: no one of that name lived there. No, they'd never heard of them. I earned my fair share of suspicious looks. One lady threatened to call the police when I insisted that someone else had lived in her house last year. I guess I was looking pretty wild by then. And all the while, the ring whispered on the edge of my hearing, its faint murmurs more than half-convincing me that I was losing my mind.

Eventually, I found my way back to the motel, sick to the stomach.

Finally! Syl said. *How long does it take a person to buy a lousy tin of tuna?*

I threw myself facedown on the bed, while she took in my tuna-less state.

Are you okay? she asked, in a very different tone. *What happened?*

"My life has disappeared," I mumbled into the pillow.

She leapt up onto the bed and batted gently at my head. *Talk sense.*

"I can't!" I wailed. "It doesn't *make* any bloody sense."

But I told her how I'd spent the last two hours. Her tail twitched, but she said nothing as I listed all the homes I'd visited, the letterboxes I'd pried into, the stores I'd scoped out. And everywhere, the same story: everyone I'd ever known had vanished into thin air.

"It's like I'm in some psycho play," I said. "The sets are

the same, but all the actors have changed, and now I don't know my lines or what I'm supposed to do. What the hell is going on? I feel like I'm going crazy."

How was I going to get answers about the ring now? Suddenly, that seemed like the least of my worries. What had happened to my mother? And all the other people I knew? It seemed insane to think that someone could have removed them without trace. Why would anyone do such a thing? Yet the other option was worse: that my powers were causing some kind of psychotic breakdown. Neither option seemed possible, yet here I was, more than halfway down the path to Crazytown—and who knew what lay at the end of that road? Today it was whispering rings. Tomorrow? I didn't want to find out.

You're not going crazy, Syl said. *Someone knows the answers. We just have to come at the problem from a different direction. You said that Adrian guy called you an Aristaean. Let's find out what he knows about that.*

Yes. I caught hold of the idea like a drowning person clutching a rope. Apart from throwing bees at my head, he hadn't seemed too bad. I sat up. "Right. I need to find him."

Sure, said Syl. *Straight after you buy me some tuna.*

6

I stopped in a dark spot between street lights, just around the corner from what I still thought of as my mother's house. I wanted to see Adrian again, and I didn't even have a last name to go on. This seemed the best place to start looking. With luck, I could catch him arriving, before he went inside and his mother realised I was there.

I still think you should just march around there and knock on her front door. Ask to see him. It could save a lot of time skulking around. Worst case is she says no, and then you can fall back on the skulking option.

"No, worst case is she calls the cops on me. That seems to be her first response to everything." My mind was only half on our conversation. Most of my attention was spreading out through the night, searching for an animal mind to use. I latched onto an owl—a different one to the one I'd thrown at Adrian's head the night before—and sent her winging through the sky to do some aerial reconnaissance for me.

She spiralled down through the night sky above my mother's street. Through her eyes, the world was sharp, every detail defined. I swooped with her along the street, the dark asphalt glistening from the rain that had fallen earlier in the evening. Her wings made no noise as we ghosted above the overhead wires.

No one was on the street. Most of the houses showed some lights, and the sounds of TV drifted on the night air, along with a hint of garlic from someone's cooking. Not even any cars moved. Well, I could be patient. The night was still young.

As she banked away on silent wings, a tiny red circle of light flared in the darkness across the street from my mother's house. Adrian's mother's house. Whoever the hell it belonged to. The light had disappeared almost immediately, but I sent her closer, and now that I knew to look for it, I saw the outline of a man in the darkness, hidden under the overgrown trees of the house opposite.

"Interesting," I said.

What is?

"Someone else is staking out the house."

Really? Are you sure?

"He's picked an odd place to smoke his cigarette if not." Even with the owl's keen vision, I wouldn't have noticed him if not for the glowing end of his cigarette. He was well hidden.

Let me go check.

"How are you going to check? You can't exactly ask him what he's doing, can you?"

He might just be waiting for his girlfriend. Or maybe he's going to rob the joint. You can't assume he's watching for this Adrian guy too.

"Actually, I thought he might be watching for me." Maybe Adrian had hired security to make sure no more crazy people broke into his mother's house. She seemed the nervous type.

Whatever. I can keep an eye on him and let you know if he calls someone or something.

"Be careful. You know how the humans around here feel about cats."

It's dark and I'm a black cat. She sauntered off with a disdainful flick of her tail. *He won't even know I'm there.*

I rode behind Syl's eyes, seeing what she saw, as she made her way around the corner, towards the house where the guy waited. She wandered into the front yard of a house several doors down from her target and leaped lightly to the top of the fence separating it from its neighbour. In this way, she slunk from yard to yard, coming at the guy from the side.

She stopped under a large rhododendron bush and

watched from concealment. The man finished his cigarette and ground it out beneath his boot, then shoved his hands in his pockets. Probably to keep them warm. It was a cold night to be standing around in someone's front yard. No lights showed in the house behind him. The residents might have been asleep, though it was kind of early for that, not even nine o'clock. Judging by the state of their garden, it was more likely that the house was empty. It had an unloved look.

Syl crept closer, but her small body must have made some rustling in the bushes, because the guy's head snapped around, and he peered into the darkness.

Jumpy little devil, isn't he? She paused, but he saw her anyway. Maybe her eyes caught the light from the streetlamps, in that creepy way that cats' eyes did, because the man's own eyes widened and he hissed.

"Scat!" He snatched up a rock and lobbed it at her. "Get the hell away from me."

Syl leapt sideways to avoid the rock—his aim was good, despite the darkness—and streaked away. *I can't believe he hissed at me.* She seemed more outraged by that than the rock.

You know what they think of cats here, I said. *They're afraid they're all shifters in disguise, come to murder them in their beds. Which, to be fair, you are.* From the safety of the next street, I could afford to laugh a little at Syl's expense.

I've never murdered anyone in their bed in my life. Her

mental tone was snippy. Clearly, she didn't find the experience as amusing as I had. She'd stopped running, and was now making her way back to another vantage point near the man. More carefully, this time.

So, you still think he's waiting for his girlfriend? I asked after a few minutes of silent observation.

You're probably right, she said. *He's most likely watching the house in case you turn up.*

Okay. Let's see what he does if I do.

Do you think that's wise? She sounded doubtful, but I was already to the corner.

I shrugged. *Let's find out.*

The thud of my boots on the sidewalk was loud in the silence. The guy had plenty of notice I was coming. I stopped outside the familiar house, not trying to hide.

Shit, he's reaching into his pocket—

I flinched and linked with Syl. We both saw him pull out a phone, and I breathed again. *Thanks for the heart attack, Syl.*

You're welcome. Next time you want me to say nothing and wait until they shoot you? She sounded grumpy.

Shhh. I wanted to listen to his conversation, but all he said was, "She's here," and hung up. I guess that answered the question of who he was watching for. The only question remaining was who was on the other end of the line. It had to be Adrian.

Did I really want to meet him now, in the dark street? Perhaps not. I stared at the overgrown garden opposite. Even though I knew he was there, it was hard to make out the figure of the man under the trees.

"Hey, mate," I called out, loud enough to be heard across the street, but not loud enough to bring the neighbours out. "Tell your boss to meet me tomorrow for breakfast at Belmonte's. Eight o'clock." If Adrian's mother had lived here any length of time he should know where that was. "Just him."

Stakeout guy made no answer.

"Yeah, you in the bushes," I said. "I know you're there. Pro tip for you: don't smoke on stakeouts. I can smell you from here."

Then I threw dignity to the winds and sprinted back up the street, towards the safety of my motel room. Would Adrian show up for breakfast? I could hardly wait to find out.

You've got to love pigeons. They're everywhere, but no one takes the slightest notice of them. It's like they're invisible. So I used them as my little eyes in the sky—and on the ground, and crapping all over the sidewalk—to watch the street outside Belmonte's, while I stayed safely ensconced in my motel room, two blocks over.

I'd started watching early—I couldn't sleep anyway, so I figured I may as well make use of my time. I'd seen the kitchen staff arrive and unlock the back entrance. Later, closer to opening time, a couple of sleepy wait staff had turned up, rugged up in scarves and overcoats against the morning chill. No one suspicious lurked out the front or watched from the upper windows of the buildings on the other side of the street.

When Adrian arrived at five to eight, the café was open with five customers inside: three waiting for takeaway coffee, and two having breakfast together at a window table. Adrian chose one of the other window tables and sat down.

He looked smart in a suit and tie. In the daylight, I could see he was older than I'd first thought, maybe early thirties. His hair was gelled within an inch of its life, making me wonder how much time he spent in front of the bathroom mirror in the mornings. I watched as he studied the menu, apparently relaxed. It seemed he'd come alone, as instructed. Good. I liked a man who did as he was told.

"I'm heading over to Belmonte's," I told Syl, shrugging into my jacket.

She was sprawled on the bed, slim black legs stretched out as far as they could go. For a small cat, she sure took up a lot of room. She opened one eye and stared up at me. *Open one of those tins before you go.*

Obediently, I opened a tin of tuna and kept my mouth

84

shut, though the urge to point out that she could easily open it herself if she would only take human form was almost overwhelming. In fact, her diet could be a lot more interesting than just tins of tuna. Syl was still good company as a cat, but I missed my friend—and I worried what would happen if she persisted in this refusal to turn human. I'd heard some horror stories about shifters who spent too much time in their animal skins, and I didn't want her ending up some feral beast.

I locked the door behind me and walked briskly to Belmonte's, hands shoved in my jacket pockets to keep them warm. The sun shone but there was no heat in it yet, and my breath made white puffs in front of my face.

It was much warmer in the café. Adrian saw me come in and rose to pull out the chair opposite his. Well, someone had been well brought up. A quick glance around as I sat down assured me that Pigeon View hadn't led me astray. The couple at the next table were nearly finished their breakfast, and they didn't look particularly threatening. Another customer had taken a table while I'd been in transit, but since she was a bent old lady, I figured I could discount her as a stooge waiting to attack me.

Adrian offered his hand before resuming his seat. "We didn't get properly introduced the other night. I'm Adrian McGovern."

"Lexi Jardine," I said, shaking his hand. His grip was

firm, and I liked his smile. He had a couple of scratches on his forehead that were probably owl-inflicted, and I felt a twinge of guilt. At least he didn't seem to be holding them against me.

"Shall we order?"

The waitress approached at a signal from him. I didn't bother checking the menu; I already knew what I was having. We ordered, and then a slightly awkward silence descended. I needed to pump him for information without giving away how ignorant I was, and I wasn't sure how to go about it.

He folded his hands on the checked tablecloth. "I'm so pleased you got in contact again. I was wondering how on earth I was going to find you."

His smile was hard to resist. The skin around his eyes crinkled into crow's feet that showed he probably smiled a lot. He certainly didn't look like the kind of guy who would spirit my mother away and take over her home.

"I'm a little surprised you *wanted* to find me after the way we met." I couldn't help smiling back. He had an open, honest face that made me want to trust him—but I'd been burned before. He'd have to do a bit more than smile appealingly to win my trust.

He laughed. "Can I tell my mother that you won't be visiting her again? She did find the experience rather alarming."

Not half as alarming as I had. But I kept the smile plastered on my face and agreed that I wouldn't be breaking into his mother's house any more.

"Do you mind if I ask what that was about?"

The waitress brought our coffees then, which gave me a minute to think. How the hell do you explain something like that? Particularly when you don't understand what the hell is going on yourself?

"I'm sorry that I scared her." I took a sip of coffee, then looked down at my cup. "I … get confused sometimes."

"Ah." He nodded, as if something had been made clear to him. "That's okay. I've heard it takes some of us like that."

Us? How many of *us* were there? My fingers tightened on the handle of my cup, and I had to force myself to relax. I didn't want to appear over-eager, but this was immense. Delicately, I sent my awareness out, probing gently. Perhaps we could have this whole conversation mind-to-mind. But there was no answer. His mind was closed to me.

I sat back, trying not to feel deflated. I could only speak mind-to-mind to shifters when they were in animal form, after all. It was probably too much to expect that I could communicate that way with other people like me.

"How long does the confusion last?" *Could* I be having some sort of psychotic episode? I'd certainly considered it, but I didn't want to believe it. My memories were *real*.

Who was I, if not the person who'd grown up in this town, spending afternoons after school gossiping with Cath Belmonte, then running home to the little house on Grosvenor Street? But how else could I make sense of what was happening? I needed more information.

"It depends," he said. "It can be hard to adjust. And it's only a little over a year since the Aristaeans were created."

Well, now he'd completely lost me. I'd had my powers as long as I could remember. Certainly longer than a year. Maybe he meant they—we?—had formed some kind of formal association a year ago?

"I can't believe I haven't met you before," he continued. "I thought I knew all the Aristaeans, but I'm sure I would remember you."

Okay, I was going to take that as a compliment. His smile was certainly warm enough. Not as appealing as Jake's smile, but then, you'd have to go a long way to find a better specimen of manhood than that hot flamethrower.

"I haven't been around much," I said, when it became obvious he was waiting for me to explain. Jake wasn't here, and this guy was. Plus he was a human like me. An Aristaean like me, too, if I could only figure out what that was. What was the point of wishing that things could have turned out differently with Jake? It would never have worked. We were too different.

"Where've you been?"

"Oh, up north." I kept it deliberately vague. This was the southernmost human city, and I didn't want to get bogged down in a detailed lie, so "north" seemed pretty safe.

"Of course." He nodded as though this information meant something. "Can I ask?" He indicated the scratches on his head with a rueful smile. "The owl? That was Cybele?"

Oh, Lord. I thought I'd been confused before. I had no idea what he was talking about. Maybe I should just admit that and beg for information. I shifted in my seat, uncomfortable with the very idea. Admitting ignorance gave him power over me, made me vulnerable—and I didn't deal well with that. I still had vivid memories of my up-close-and-personal acquaintance with the inside of a police cell in this very neighbourhood. I did *not* want to end up back there if this guy decided there was something fishy about me.

I gave a casual shrug, still smiling, and hoped he'd leave it alone. But I filed the name away for later. Cybele. Who or what was Cybele?

He held his hands up. "Fine, you don't want to say. A mystery woman, huh?" He shook his head. "Funny, I thought I knew all the multis. Apparently not."

Okay, that was enough. Multis? My head was spinning. Time to do some digging.

"So, what do you do?" I asked, indicating the suit and power tie. Maybe if I got him talking, I'd get answers to some of my questions.

"I'm a lawyer for EmeryCorp."

"And that keeps you busy?"

"It certainly does. It's a great job, something different all the time. We have a lot of construction going on at the moment. Mrs Emery is on a one-woman crusade to improve the standard of living here in Newport. If we're not building public housing, we're funding education programs in our schools, or overseeing the efforts of half a dozen charities. The Emery Foundation is particularly concerned with bettering the lives of women."

That sounded like a plan I could get behind. Maybe that shiny new building at my old school had been funded by his boss. "Mrs Emery must be very rich." If she could afford to do all that, it sounded like shaper-level rich, though obviously she couldn't be a shaper, not in the human territories.

"She is, although it's not all charity work. There's the Foundation, which handles the charity side, and then there's EmeryCorp, where I work. She's a very persuasive lady, and she's managed to talk a lot of big investors into joining her in developing things like shopping centres and office complexes." He grinned. "I think she could talk a man into selling his own mother. But seriously, Newport is lucky to have her. She's making a difference in so many lives."

Including his, perhaps. That suit looked expensive. "I've never heard of her before. Is she new in town?"

"Yes. EmeryCorp's headquarters is in Bourneville, but the heat didn't agree with her, so she's moved down here. Bourneville's loss is our gain."

"She sounds wonderful."

"She is." He flashed that warm smile again. "I bet she'd love to meet you, too—a new Aristaean in town. She likes to keep tabs on us."

Whoa. This Mrs Emery was one of us too?

He drained the last of his coffee and set the cup back down in the saucer. "Look—tonight's the opening of our new women's shelter. Mrs Emery will be there, and I can introduce you. Will you come? I don't want to lose track of you again."

Thank God. I wouldn't have to stalk him. "Sure. That sounds great."

He laughed. "Well, I don't know about *great*. The speeches might be dull, but at least they'll be short, and the catering team usually does a good job. Where should I pick you up?"

"How about I meet you at your mother's house?" He seemed like a nice guy, but I wasn't going to tell him where I was staying. The habit of distrusting people was strong. It had also saved my butt a couple of times.

"So mysterious!" he said.

"Always."

7

The only good thing about having my whole life disappear like smoke on the wind was that I'd also lost the baggage that came with it. No one looked sideways at me on the street, or whispered about me behind my back. No one crossed to the other side of the road when they saw me coming. I didn't earn any extra attention from the police. I could hardly believe it the first time a patrol car passed me and it didn't slow down for a closer look. It was as if I were invisible.

Worry for my mother still nagged at the back of my mind, but I blocked it off, trying to focus on what I could control. Which wasn't much, since Adrian and his Aristaean friends looked like my only leads at the moment, but I was determined to make a good impression.

The look in his eyes told me I'd succeeded. It was just starting to get dark when I arrived outside my mother's house. His car, a powerful-looking silver sedan, was already waiting at the kerb, and he got out as I approached.

"You look lovely." He leaned in to brush his lips across my cheek, enveloping me in the sandalwood scent of his aftershave.

"Thanks."

The dress was new, since I hadn't brought anything with me that was suitable for going out. It was sleeveless, barely covering the tattoo on my left shoulder blade. The soft black fabric flared gently out from my hips. It probably would have looked better with strappy black sandals, but I wore it with my boots, as the budget didn't stretch to new shoes as well. At this rate I'd have to get a job soon, as my cash reserves were dwindling fast. Maybe I'd apply at Belmonte's again and show that taciturn waitress a thing or two about customer service.

Adrian opened the passenger door of his car for me. Such a gentleman. It was warm inside, and I sank into the soft leather seats with a sigh of pleasure. It beat driving around in Joe's poor battered truck with the cold air blasting in through the holes in the roof. Plus I had to wrestle with the door every time just to get it to open.

I hoped Joe was using mine. I felt guilty about his truck—I'd never meant to be away this long, and I'd certainly never meant to return it all beat up and covered in giant dog slobber. But some things you didn't get a choice about.

I'd been jumpy ever since I'd arrived, always looking over my shoulder for that damned dog. So far there'd been no sign of him. Did that mean that Hades had given up the chase? Or was Cerberus still obeying my command to stop following me? I could hardly believe someone like me could command Hades' hell hound—but he *was* an animal, after all, and my gift had never failed me yet.

Adrian kept up a flow of conversation as he drove, about his work, and the opening we were going to.

"Will there be many other Aristaeans there?" I asked.

"Yes, a few. Might be some familiar faces for you."

I made a non-committal noise. By this point, I held very little hope of finding anyone I recognised in this city. I was starting to wonder if Adrian was right and I was suffering from some weird confusion brought on by becoming an Aristaean—and that I'd imagined my whole past. My heart cried out against that explanation, but my brain was having a lot of trouble coming up with a better one. Syl said if I was going to imagine a whole past, I should at least have imagined one where everyone adored me, instead of one where I was almost universally reviled. She had a point. It gave me hope that I wasn't going crazy.

Twenty minutes later, we arrived. I wasn't familiar with the area, but it was pretty rundown, more like the Newport

I remembered. No new shopping complexes or fancy school buildings here. The street was full of cars but Adrian miraculously found a parking spot close to the new women's refuge, which was housed in an old converted warehouse. New glass doors had been fitted to the entry, and their handles were tied together with a giant pink bow. People milled on the sidewalk in front of the doors, clearly waiting for something.

That something proved to be a long, dark limousine, which pulled into the kerb in front of the doors a few moments later.

"Here she is," Adrian said, a smile lighting his face.

A man in a dinner suit hopped out of the front seat and held open the back door. An elegant leg that ended in a stiletto heel appeared, followed by the rest of a slim, white-haired woman. Without those heels, she wouldn't have come up to my shoulder. Her dress was a simple black sheath, but its cut screamed money. Her face was relatively unlined. She looked mid-fifties—sixty, tops. The famous Mrs Emery, I assumed.

She strode confidently in those towering heels across the sidewalk to the doors. An aide handed her a giant pair of scissors and she turned to face the gathered crowd.

"I won't keep you standing out here in the cold for long." She beamed at the little knot of people, who murmured appreciatively. "But just think for a moment about how cold it is out here on the street, and imagine if you had nowhere else to go. Women deserve better than that. Everyone does. This shelter is just the start. EmeryCorp and The Emery Foundation are going to make this city great. We will build a haven for humanity, where no one will live in poverty. Every child will have a home and an education, and no one will have to live in fear." She hefted the giant scissors, and cut cleanly through the ribbon on the doors. "I hereby declare the Emery Women's Shelter open."

The crowd clapped enthusiastically as Mrs Emery thrust open the doors and led the way inside. Beyond the small reception area was a much larger room where waiters offered trays of drinks and canapés.

"This is the communal lounge," Adrian said. "They'll move the furniture in tomorrow. It was the only room big enough for tonight. The rest of the shelter is mainly bedrooms and bathrooms, with a couple of offices. Oh, and the kitchen, of course."

"Uh-huh."

An underwater scene was painted on one wall, with smiling fish and friendly-looking octopi. Adrian noticed me looking at it.

"We've put a lot of thought into making this a welcoming and homey place. There'll be a lot of toys in here for the kids. Leaving home is a scary time for them."

He sounded as proud as if he'd painted the mural himself. The project was obviously dear to his heart.

"It's lovely," I said.

"Let me get you a drink." He snagged two champagnes from a passing waiter and offered me one. "Oh, there's Bruno and Irene. Come, and I'll introduce you."

He took my arm and steered me toward a couple on the other side of the room. The man's dark hair was shot through with grey, and he was considerably older than the blonde hanging on his arm. A daughter? Work colleague, perhaps?

"Lexi, I'd like you to meet Bruno Grasso and his wife, Irene."

Okay, not his daughter, then. Probably the right age for it, though. Bruno shook my hand, but Irene only fluttered her fingers at me in a languid wave. Her fingernails were red, and so long I wondered how she did anything for herself. Picking her nose must be hell.

"And this is Matt," Adrian added as another man joined the group.

"Hi." Matt shook my hand enthusiastically. He looked about the same age as Adrian—late twenties, early thirties. "Nice of you to come. These work things are usually deadly dull."

"You all work together?"

"We're the shining lights of EmeryCorp's legal division,"

he said. "Except for Irene. I don't know what she does all day. Shops, probably."

Bruno laughed and patted Irene's hand indulgently. "We have an equal division of labour in our household. I make the money, she spends it."

Irene said nothing, though the look she gave Matt wasn't friendly. Hopefully she wasn't one of the Aristaeans. I didn't particularly want to get to know her better.

Mrs Emery joined the group. She was the shortest person there, even in her towering heels, but she had that indefinable something that made her the immediate centre of attention. The men all straightened their shoulders, and even Irene smiled.

"Mrs Emery, may I introduce my friend, Lexi?"

Her attention had almost a physical weight. She offered her hand, her wrist circled by a chunky silver cuff, and her handshake was as firm as Bruno's had been. "Any friend of Adrian's is most welcome." Her eyes raked over me, taking in my hair, my dress, the way I stood.

A waiter appeared with a tray of canapés.

"Something to eat?" Adrian said.

As I turned toward him a hand flicked at my shoulder.

"Sorry," said Mrs Emery. "I thought you had a spider on your back. What is that?"

I tugged at the shoulder of my dress. The armholes were cut away so deep that the edge of my tattoo kept peeking out as I moved. "Just my tattoo."

"You have a tattoo?" Adrian asked. "What is it—a butterfly?"

"An archer."

Mrs Emery pushed my dress aside to expose my tattoo. "Very nice." She ran a finger over it and I shivered. It felt like something was crawling on my skin. She looked expectantly at Adrian. "Have you given Lexi the tour of the facility yet?"

"I was just about to," he said.

"Good." She smiled. "Lexi, you must come to my gala on Friday night."

Adrian's shoulders relaxed, as if this was the signal he'd been waiting for. He turned to me with a huge smile. "I'm sure she'd love to, wouldn't you, Lexi?"

"Umm, sure." If it meant the other Aristaeans accepted me, I was all for it. "That's very kind of you."

"Excellent!" She turned to Bruno, and I felt as if I'd just been released from the principal's office, relieved to be out from under her scrutiny. They started discussing something to do with taxes, and Adrian smiled at me.

"Let me show you around."

"Sure."

We went back out to the reception area and down the hall behind it. We peeked into the dining room and the kitchen, which was buzzing with people preparing food, and waiters hurrying back and forth.

"Down here are the staff offices, and that way are the suites."

Suite was a grand name, but the reality was less imposing: a bedroom painted in cheerful yellow, with two single beds and a small wardrobe, and not much else. A tiny bathroom with a shower and toilet opened off it. The next room held two double bunks instead of single beds, but was otherwise much the same. Not exactly palatial, but I suppose if you were a woman fleeing a violent partner with your children, you'd be grateful for a place that was clean and safe. And Adrian had explained that the shelter was more than just temporary accommodation: it also provided things like legal assistance and helped find permanent accommodation.

I could have done with something like this myself, though it was a shaper I'd needed shelter from, not an ex. I had a feeling these cheerful yellow walls couldn't have done much to save me from Erik Anders. I stroked the blue and yellow bedspread on the top bunk wistfully. Not all shapers were that bad, as it turned out.

We peeked into a couple more rooms, then Adrian's phone rang. "Excuse me a minute." He spoke briefly to the person on the other end, then turned to me. "Sorry, I have to take this. Have a look around; I'll only be a minute."

"That's okay. I'll just visit the bathroom."

I headed back down the corridor toward the kitchen; there'd been a sign for toilets down there. A tall waiter came toward me with an empty tray and, before I'd had time to wonder why he was walking away from the kitchen with an empty tray instead of a full one, he'd shoved open the toilet door and bundled me inside.

My God, it was as if thinking of shapers had summoned one. My heart did a glad little leap as I realised it was Jake.

He looked good, his hair just brushing the collar of his dinner suit. I'd never seen him so formally dressed. He looked fit and strong, though I suppose that jacket might have been hiding some bandages. It was only a few days since he'd been shot.

"I might have known I'd find you here," he said, his mouth a bitter twist.

I jerked my gaze away from contemplation of his powerful shoulders and realised his blue eyes were colder than an Arctic winter, and he was holding that tray as if he meant to use it as a weapon. Not a happy reunion, then.

"What's that supposed to mean?"

"You, in the middle of a bloody One World convention. I knew I shouldn't have trusted you."

Ouch. That stung.

"For God's sake, Jake, it's the opening of a women's refuge, and they're not One Worlders. Just a bunch of businessmen in suits. What is this obsession with One Worlders?"

And what the hell was a fireshaper doing in human territory? If those people out there found out what he was …

Well, to be honest, if they found out what he was, they would probably be the ones going down, rather than him. Though, as we'd already demonstrated this week, fireshapers were just as vulnerable to bullets as regular humans. Either way it would be an ugly scene. Definitely one to be avoided.

He loomed over me. "Did you come running to your friends as soon as you got it? I can't believe I played right into your hands. You couldn't wait to get out of Berkley's Bay, could you?"

I squared my shoulders, though he was scaring me. If looks could kill, I'd be a corpse already. "What are you talking about?"

"I don't have time for your bullshit," he ground out through gritted teeth. "Where. Is. The. Ring?"

"What ring?" It was getting harder to look him in the eyes.

He caught me by the shoulders, his fingers digging into my flesh, and shook me. "Cut it out. There's only one ring that matters."

I held up my hand to display the plain gold band that adorned my finger. "This is the only ring I have."

And I wasn't even lying.

"Zeus's balls, you've given it to them already, haven't you? Give me one good reason why I shouldn't kill you." Tiny flames sprang to life and licked up and down his arms, as if he could barely control the blaze that raged within. Pure terror held me transfixed as I stared into the fire leaping in his eyes. He would kill me right here, in this gleaming new bathroom, if I didn't talk fast.

I tried to twist out of his reach, but there was no escaping his iron grip. The Jake who'd smiled at me, who'd fought at my side and kissed me, was gone. Only the Master of the South-east remained, the fireshaper who sat on the Ruby Council and dispensed justice as he saw fit. That man had no mercy.

I laid my hands flat against his hard chest. "Whoa, there. You're looking for the ring we took from the Adept? Last time I saw it, you had it. Why would you think I took it?" It took everything I had to keep my voice casual, as if he hadn't just threatened to kill me—a threat I was convinced he would carry out with no remorse.

"Because when I woke up in hospital it was gone, and you'd done a runner. Pretty interesting coincidence, wouldn't you say?"

"My mother was sick—I had to rush home. Didn't Joe tell you?"

Doubt flickered in his eyes, but they soon hardened again. "If your mother's so sick, why are you out partying with the One Worlders?"

"It turned out not to be as serious as they first thought. And will you give it a rest with the One World accusations?"

"It's not an accusation. I *know*. I've seen some of these people before. That woman is dangerous."

"Who, Mrs Emery?" The way she'd stared at me had kind of freaked me out, but that didn't make her dangerous, just a little creepy. *He* was far more dangerous than anyone else in this building. "Yeah, she seems terrifying, going around supporting victims of domestic violence and constructing new buildings for schools."

"You don't know what you're talking about." His tone was flat, almost tired, but finally, his flames died away. "You should leave now, before they suck you into their schemes and it's too late. Or before I change my mind. Hades told me not to kill you, but he didn't say I had to keep you in one piece."

I'd have to remember to thank Hades for that next time I saw him. But Jake was kidding himself if he thought I could let this go now. Wild horses couldn't drag me away. I was *this* close to finally getting answers to a mystery that had plagued me all my life. And I wasn't convinced that Adrian didn't know what had happened to my mother. No, there was no way I was leaving now, just because Jake bloody Steele had some wild conspiracy theory going.

The door opened, nearly hitting him in the back, and a woman entered, startled to find the two of us exchanging glares at three paces.

I smiled at her. "It's a unisex bathroom. We're just leaving."

I brushed past Jake. He made no move to stop me, though I could feel his gaze burning into the back of my head until the door closed behind me. Or maybe that was just my conscience talking. I wasn't sure if I'd convinced him I didn't have the ring, but at least his murderous rage had cooled.

It occurred to me, as I went looking for Adrian, that maybe I should just give the damn thing to Jake. It didn't look as though I'd be showing it to my mother any time soon, and if he was willing to chase me into human territory for it, it must be hugely important to him. But the comment about killing me rankled. I'd thought I was a little more important to him than that. Maybe he didn't *deserve* the stupid ring.

I clung to the hope that the mysterious Aristaeans would have answers for me, about the ring and everything else. I just had to find a way to ask the right questions.

8

I woke up suffocating, a weight pressing on my throat. I thrashed and flailed my way out of the sheets and sat bolt upright, panting.

Good morning to you too. Syl glared at me from the floor, her mental tone laden with disgust. *What is your problem?*

She jumped back onto the bed and I touched my throat, my heart still hammering. My skin was warm. She must have been lying across my neck. Bloody cat.

"My problem? What's yours? How about a little personal space?" She behaved so much like a cat it was hard to remember she was actually a person sometimes. "There's another bed there you could use."

I was cold. She began licking one delicate paw, as if that settled the matter. *How was your party?* She'd been asleep when I'd come in last night. I'd had to shift her off my pillow.

"It wasn't a party." That made it sound like I'd been out getting shitfaced. "It was an opening."

Party, opening. Potato, potahto. Did you meet any other bee dudes?

"No, but I'm going to a gala with Adrian tomorrow night. He said there would be some Aristaeans there." Hopefully there would be a chance for some private conversation, and I'd finally get a few questions answered. "You'll never guess who I saw last night."

Your mum?

"No." Though it was almost as strange. "Jake."

Hot flamethrower dude? What was he doing there?

I sighed. "Looking for the ring."

We both glanced at the innocent-looking gold band on my finger. I'd gotten so used to its constant whispering in the back of my mind whenever I wore it that I hardly noticed it anymore. I'd been wearing it non-stop for the last few days, too scared of losing it to leave it behind when I went out or to keep it in my pocket. My finger was the safest place for it.

I assume he wasn't throwing fire around. It's pretty risky, isn't it, for him to be in a place like this? If they knew he was a fireshaper ...

"Well, exactly. Who knows what would happen? Not that he seems to care."

Yeah, but this ring must be serious shit for him to take a risk like that.

Well, I guess we already knew that. If it belonged to the god Apollo, it obviously had power. I wish I knew why Erik Anders had been so keen to get his grubby paws on it, or what it had to do with these mysterious shadow shapers Jake and Hades were so worried about, but first I needed my own questions about it answered.

"I'll give it back to him, I promise." I did feel a twinge of guilt—just a twinge—that my stealing it had forced Jake to follow me somewhere that was so dangerous for him. But then I remembered the death threats and hardened my heart again. "Just as soon as I get some information from these Aristaeans."

But that could be a while, given the current rate of progress. She tipped her head on one side and regarded me doubtfully.

"Such faith! Tomorrow night. It's not long to wait."

And what did dear Jacob say when you told him you didn't have the ring?

"He took a little convincing," I admitted. "He certainly didn't seem happy. In fact, he started throwing wild accusations around. Said Adrian and his friends are One Worlders."

Syl's lip curled back in a silent snarl. *Those arseholes. I wouldn't piss on them if they were on fire. Is he right? Because we don't want anything to do with them if he is.*

She didn't want anything to do with anyone. But we

didn't all have the luxury of hiding away, waiting for someone else to bring us food. "They seem to be all about building a better world. They're doing a lot of good for this city, as far as I can see." If that made them One Worlders, then maybe the One World organisation wasn't as bad as I'd always believed.

Syl stretched, her front claws digging into my hip.

"Ow! Cut that out."

She gave me that insolent look that cats do so well, and slowly retracted her claws.

I threw back the blankets and got up. "Why can't you be a human for a change?" I pulled my jeans on in swift, savage movements. "This cat thing is really starting to get to me."

Her green eyes stared at me, unblinking. *I'm a cat. Get used to it.*

"No, you're *not*." I wanted to punch something. Pity Jake wasn't handy. "You're a cat shifter who never shifts. You'll end up a feral moggy if you don't cut it out, and I'm sick of you pretending there's nothing wrong. You're just ignoring a whole side of yourself, losing a huge chunk of your life."

Her tail twitched. *I'm ignoring things? What about you?*

"What's that supposed to mean?"

You're out partying, instead of solving the mystery you came here to solve. Your past has gone missing, your own mother's disappeared, you've got a stolen magic ring on your finger, but you'd rather hang with Adrian the bee dude than go looking for answers.

I zipped my jacket, the sound loud in the quiet room. How dared she? I'd done nothing but look for answers, and what had she done? Lain around on the bed and waited for me to feed her. "I didn't ask you to come. I'm sure Holly and Joe would have been happy to keep you supplied with tuna."

I left, slamming the door behind me. If she got hungry, she'd just have to turn human and open her own damn tins.

Still fuming, I strode down the street. I was hungry, but I was sick of Belmonte's and all its reminders of a past that was lost to me, so I grabbed a croissant from a bakery and munched as I walked.

How could I prove that I wasn't crazy? My ID papers didn't list an address, only that I was a registered citizen of Newport. What about a birth certificate? My parents had been living in that house when my brother and I were born, so my birth certificate would prove to Adrian and his mother that I had once lived there, at least. It would also prove my mother's existence.

Feeling energised by a new goal, I caught the train into the business district of town, where all the government offices were. Bright sunshine fell on my head as I emerged from the underground railway system. The city seemed cleaner than usual, without the trash I was used to seeing piling up against the walls of buildings. Several giant cranes poked up above the skyline—a rash of new buildings were springing up. Most of the cranes sported the EmeryCorp logo, a giant entwined E and C. Maybe it was my imagination, but the people I passed on the street seemed to walk with more of a spring in their step than I remembered. The whole place had an air of prosperity that I'd only associated before with the shaper cities.

I passed a big electronics retailer, its windows sparkling in the sun. A bank of TVs in the windows were all showing the same cat food commercial, which reminded me how cranky I was with Syl. I glared at the fluffy, white kitten on the screens. Shifters who went too far into their animal sides sometimes lost their humanity altogether, becoming nothing but beasts. How could I keep Syl from going down that path when she wouldn't even admit she had a problem?

I was still looking at the kitten when big red letters flashed up on every screen: BEWARE RING.

What the hell? The words had only been there for a split second. The cute kitten was still prancing adorably around some woman's ankles as she spooned cat food into a gleaming bowl. What did *beware ring* have to do with a cat food commercial? It didn't make any sense. Had I imagined the whole thing?

By this time, I'd stopped walking and was staring into

the shop window, eyes glued to the nearest TV. The cat food ad finished and the program resumed, something about nature judging by the beautiful aerial shots of pine forests and a sparkling river snaking its way through the trees. Just as I was starting to feel silly for standing there waiting, more red letters appeared. They were there and gone again so quickly I might have missed them if I hadn't been watching so carefully, but it definitely wasn't my imagination. They were real, and they said: GET IT APOLLO.

What was this? Some kind of joke? I glanced around, half-expecting to spot a hidden camera filming my reactions. Was I being pranked for some stupid reality show? But even as I had the thought, I knew that wasn't it. These messages were way too specific. If it had been a prank, they would have said, HEY, YOU, YOUR FLY'S UNDONE or something equally infantile. *Get it Apollo* was more like a text message from the universe, urging me to action.

I stroked the ring with my thumb, as if to assure myself it was still there. *Well, hey, universe, that seems like a great idea, but a few details wouldn't go astray.* Where *was* Apollo? How was I meant to find a god on my own? I waited there another ten minutes, to see if any other messages flashed up, but the screens didn't bring me any more texts. Maybe the universe hadn't paid its phone bill.

I continued walking, more slowly than before, feeling chilled despite the sunshine. It was as if someone was watching me. How could they know I would be next to that shop at that moment to see the messages otherwise? And how could anyone put messages on the TV like that? Had everyone watching that channel seen them too? I had a feeling the answer to that one was *no*, which made the whole thing even creepier. I was messing around in something big, caught in the middle of powers I didn't understand.

Maybe I should give the damn ring to Jake. Was that what the message meant? Was that how I was meant to give it to Apollo? It seemed like a fireshaper might have a better idea than I would of how to find a god.

Once I'd spoken to the Aristaeans tomorrow night, maybe I'd do that. I was sick of the ring's whispering, sick of everyone being mad at me. I didn't know where Jake was, but he probably wouldn't be far away. I was pretty sure he knew I was lying when I said I didn't know what had happened to the ring. He'd be back, and when I saw him again, I'd hand the cursed thing over straight away and wash my hands of the whole stupid mess.

My feet had brought me to the steps of the Registry of Births, Deaths, and Marriages. It was one of the oldest buildings in town, and more fancy than most in the human territories, built in the hope-filled days after the great wars ended, when it seemed possible that life could be more than a hard-scrabble fight for existence. I trod up the worn sandstone steps, feeling lighter now the decision was made.

Inside was less attractive than the exterior. The interior was painted the drab grey of government buildings everywhere, staffed by workers who rarely smiled. I filled in the form to request a copy of my birth certificate and got in line to show my ID and pay the fee. Then I waited on the hard seats while the request was processed.

It took a long time. More than half an hour had passed, and dozens of people had come and gone, their business completed, before a bored-looking woman called my name. She pushed my form back across the counter at me.

"I'm sorry, we have no record of any such birth."

I glanced down at the form in confusion. My name—Alexia Jardine—was printed there in my own handwriting, along with my date and place of birth. Everything was correct.

"But you must have a record—I was born here."

She sighed, as if I was putting a great burden on her. "Show me your ID."

I'd already shown it to another member of staff when I'd put the form in—they didn't issue birth certificates to anyone but the person themselves or their parents. She looked it over carefully, comparing the photo to my face, and checking it against the details on the form.

"Well, it *looks* legitimate," she said, her tone managing to imply that it couldn't possibly be.

Great. Was I a suspected criminal now? I breathed a sigh of relief when she handed my ID back. For a moment, I'd been afraid she'd accuse me of having fake ID and call the cops on me.

"But I'm afraid it's not on the database," she added, as if that closed the matter.

"There must be a mistake," I insisted, fighting down a panicky feeling of déjà vu. It was happening again. *I'm standing right here! I exist!* "Can you look again?"

"If it's not on the database, it's not on the database." She heaved another sigh, as if explaining things to a two-year-old. "Looking again won't make any difference. You could ask for a search of the original paper records, but they're in storage in the archives. It takes two weeks and the fee is five hundred dollars."

Five hundred dollars! I didn't have that kind of money.

"No, thank you," I said, and turned away.

I walked back out into the sunshine. The sky above was still blue; the throngs of people still strode purposefully down the street.

The only thing that had changed was that, officially, I didn't exist.

9

I wore the same dress that I'd bought to go to the opening, since my budget didn't allow for multiple clothing purchases in the same week. I figured you couldn't go far wrong with a little black dress.

Everything else could go wrong, of course. I mustered a smile for Adrian as I climbed into his silver car again, though I didn't feel much like smiling. Discovering that I didn't officially exist had thrown me into a funk that was hard to shake off. The fact that Syl was barely talking to me didn't help either. Nor did the fact that I was no closer to finding my mother. I'd spent most of the day wandering aimlessly around our old neighbourhood, hoping to somehow spot someone I recognised. I hated feeling so helpless. A permanent anxious knot had lodged itself beneath my breastbone. At this point, I would almost have welcomed running into Jake again. Fighting with him would at least let off some steam.

This party gave me the illusion that I was doing something. Action, movement—anything was better than staring at the ceiling of my motel room, or walking the streets until my feet begged for mercy.

"You know," Adrian said, breaking into my gloomy thoughts, "picking you up on the street outside my mother's house like this could give a man a complex. Don't you trust me?"

I figured saying no would be rude, so I smiled and said nothing.

"You should," he said, when he realised I wasn't going to reply. "We're on the same side."

"Which side would that be?"

"Humanity's, of course. This is a big dream we're part of. No more children living in poverty, everyone given the opportunities to climb as high as they're able: to create, or to build, to live the life they've dreamed of. Imagine what that would be like." His voice was full of enthusiasm.

"Sounds wonderful."

"It will be. I firmly believe that we will get there. Education and jobs for all who want them. That's the future we're building through the work of the Foundation. Take a look out there." He gestured out the window. We were passing through the business district of town. "In ten years' time you won't recognise the place. EmeryCorp and its business partners are revolutionising this city: more office space, more hotels, more shopping centres. This will be the biggest city on the Eastern Seaboard, the economic heart of the continent."

Really? He might have to destroy a couple of shaper cities before he could make that claim, but it was a nice dream. And it certainly wouldn't hurt to bring more prosperity to the human territories. I could see the difference EmeryCorp had made already, in the year since I'd last been here.

"Sounds like Mrs Emery has big plans."

"Oh, she does." He grinned at me, like a little child in his excitement. It was nice to see someone who cared so much about his work. He lowered his voice. "And tonight will be another step forward. More of us will be created."

Us? "You mean Aristaeans?"

He laughed, as if I'd made a joke. "No. They'll probably be called Zephyrs. Not that it affects you, of course, with two already. You wouldn't want to be greedy, would you?"

I smiled and agreed that I wouldn't, though I didn't have the faintest idea what he was talking about. What did I already have two of? I mean, apart from the obvious. He hadn't been making sexual allusions.

He joined a freeway that left the city proper and headed out into the farmlands surrounding it.

"Where are we going?" I'd assumed the gala would be

somewhere in the city, but it didn't look like it. The engine purred as he put his foot down.

"Mrs Emery's estate. You'll love it."

When we arrived twenty minutes later, I had to admit that the property was spectacular.

"It used to be a winery," Adrian said as we turned into a long, winding driveway. Lamp posts spaced along each side lit the way, and fairy lights decorated the graceful trees arranged in artful groups on the manicured lawn. Off to the right, some distance from the house, a small number of vines stood in neat rows.

"Doesn't look like she'd get much of a harvest now."

"They're just for decoration these days. Mrs E says they remind her of home."

I didn't know where she'd lived before, but her current digs made my little apartment above the bookshop look pretty sad. The driveway wound its way up to the house, which was simply enormous, and performed a graceful circle in front of it. A whole bunch of expensive-looking cars were parked off to the side in neat rows on the grass. Looked like there was quite a crowd tonight.

We pulled up in front of the imposing entry, and a young man in uniform stepped forward and opened my door, offering a white-gloved hand to help me out of the car. A little flustered by the attention, I got out, feeling as fancy as a shaper arriving at a council meeting. Adrian joined me and handed the car keys to the young man, who bowed and got into the driver's seat, presumably to add the car to the ranks already parked on the lawn.

Adrian offered his arm, and I laid a hand on it as we walked up the steps.

"It all seems very … formal," I said.

Another attendant sprang to open the heavy front doors for us, and practically stood at attention as we passed inside.

He grinned. "Mrs E knows how to throw a party."

He led me to a room that was two storeys high. A massive fireplace stood at one end, the stones of its chimney a feature all the way up the wall to the distant ceiling. Flames leapt in the fireplace, and the room was pleasantly warm. Little knots of people stood scattered about, drinking champagne and chatting. The buzz of their conversation filled the air. There must have been close to a hundred people there, but the room was so big that it wasn't at all crowded.

Adrian guided me gently through them all, saying hello and introducing me here and there, stopping for a longer chat with some, but always moving. He seemed to know everyone in the room. Names whizzed past me, never to be remembered, and I soon gave up trying, exchanging smiles and pleasantries until my face ached from smiling.

My attention wandered to the floor-to-ceiling windows all along one wall. The terrace outside was softly lit, and a few guests braved the chill out there, mostly smokers. Beyond the terrace, the land fell away sharply to an ornamental lake framed by more picturesque trees. Whoever had designed the landscaping here had certainly earned their money. It was the prettiest place I'd ever seen. In autumn, some of those trees would be spectacular.

A new voice cut into my thoughts. "Hey! I was hoping Adrian would bring you again."

It was Matt, Adrian's workmate, who I'd met at the opening of the women's shelter.

"Hi, Matt. Nice to see you. Are Bruno and Irene here too?"

"Of course. They wouldn't miss a night like this. They're out on the terrace." He rolled his eyes. "I was out there, too, but Bruno wouldn't stop talking work, so I had to escape. Please take pity on me and talk about something else."

I laughed. "Sure. What would you like to talk about?"

"Anything. Just don't mention the words *contract* or *billable hours*, or I won't be responsible for my actions."

That was the best offer I'd had in days. I cast a sidelong glance at Adrian; he was deep in conversation with two older men who from their conversation appeared to be bankers, and wasn't paying any attention to Matt and me. "Are you an Aristaean?"

He looked at me as if he thought I should have already

known the answer. "No. Adrian told us you were, though. There are a couple here tonight."

"Really?"

"Mrs Emery is very generous," he said, which seemed like a non sequitur, but I was trying not to give away how very ignorant I was, which made this conversation tricky. He gave me a quizzical look. "Don't you know who your fellow chosen are? You were all there together."

If only I could just come straight out and ask him what the hell he was talking about. But the habit of hiding my abilities had become so ingrained that I couldn't open myself up like that. My brother had died because the wrong people had found out what I could do. Holly had nearly died, too, because Erik Anders had wanted to use my power. Any time I talked about it, someone got hurt.

These people seemed like me, but a couple of little things weren't adding up. What did this talk of creating Zephyrs mean? And if Adrian and these others were all Aristaeans, how could they have come into their powers only a year ago, when I'd had mine all my life?

"I've been suffering from a bit of confusion lately," I said now to Matt. Adrian had bought that excuse, and it was convenient. Maybe it was even true, considering the disappearance of everyone I'd ever known, but I still wasn't ready to admit that my whole life history was a lie. Something else was going on here, and I was damned if I was going to admit anything I didn't have to until I figured out what it was. "I can't even remember how many of us there are."

"Only about sixty, I believe." He spoke softly, so I had to lean close to hear him over the noise of the other conversations in the room. "Aristaeus wasn't all that strong."

Aristaeus was a person? What the hell?

Before I could ask any more, Adrian cut into our conversation. "It's time for dinner, folks. Let's head into the dining room."

The dining room proved to be another enormous, high-ceilinged room, with a feature fireplace that matched the one at the other end of the house. This one wasn't lit, however. Instead, the hum of ducted air-conditioning formed a barely perceptible background beneath the noise of conversation, and the fireplace boasted an arrangement of pine cones and dried flowers.

A dozen round tables, laden with white linen and glassware, took up half the room. Almost as soon as we found our seats, the waiters brought out the first course, which was smoked salmon. A little more upmarket than my usual diet. Bruno and Irene were at our table, as well as Matt, who seemed permanently dateless, and several other people whose names I forgot as soon as Adrian introduced them. The men all wore expensive-looking suits, and the women were uniformly sleek. There was enough gold jewellery in the room to keep a thief in champagne and caviar for years.

I had no more opportunity for private conversation with Matt as the table talk turned to business. I said as little as possible and focused on the food, which was delicious, as the waiters brought out more and more courses. Wine flowed freely, too, though I was careful not to take too much, and the chatter grew louder and more animated as the evening wore on.

Mrs Emery was seated at a table close to the fireplace, but dessert came and went without any movement from her, so it seemed we wouldn't have to sit through any speeches tonight. Adrian noticed the direction of my gaze and leaned closer.

"See the guy on Mrs E's left?" I nodded. "That's Nick Crawshaw, the owner of Hellsham Press." Even I'd heard of Hellsham Press: they published the biggest newspaper in the city. "And the guy on her other side is John Hanrahan, the property developer. Next to him is Mike Newton. He's the CEO of EmeryCorp. My ultimate boss."

The man in question was just another balding businessman in a suit.

"I thought Mrs Emery was the boss?"

"Mike looks after the day-to-day running of the business. Mrs E doesn't bother with the small stuff. She's more a big-picture kind of person."

"She seems to know a lot of powerful people." I'd never heard of the property developer guy, but from the size of the sapphire flashing on his little finger, I gathered he wasn't short of cash. And I knew Nick Crawshaw was a gazillionaire. "Who are the others at her table? Are they all bigshots too?"

"You could say that. They've all signed onto the team, so tonight's really about rewarding them." He gave me a meaningful nod.

It took my brain a minute to work through that one. "You mean they're becoming … Zephyrs?"

I'd spoken softly, but Irene, seated on Adrian's other side, turned her head sharply at that. "You told her?"

"Relax. She's one of us. A multi."

If anything, Irene's glare became icier. "She's not joining us tonight, is she?"

"We're not shapers," he said. "There's no point replacing one monopoly with another. We need to spread the love around."

"Good. I've waited long enough. I don't want my reward diluted."

At that point, Mrs Emery got up to make a speech after all, but I didn't listen. I was too busy going over the conversation in my head, with the feeling of being an actor in a play where everyone else knew their lines but I was madly ad-libbing. Unfortunately, the little hints I was getting were adding up to a picture I didn't like the look of.

From the sounds of it, Adrian and his friends had found a way to give ordinary people powers. There seemed to be different sorts, with different names. A year ago, someone called Aristaeus had created the Aristaeans, which was apparently what both Adrian and I were—but he'd also mentioned something about Cybele ...

None of it meshed with my memories or my own feeling about my powers. Tonight, Irene and the favoured few would become Zephyrs, whatever they were. I needed more information, but I was starting to think I'd been right not to reveal too much about myself. Something very odd was going on here, and I had a sinking feeling that I knew what it was.

When the speech was over, the lights dimmed and the dancing started. Matt insisted I join him on the dance floor despite my protests that I was a terrible dancer. Fortunately, only basic shuffling was required and I circled mindlessly in his arms, watching Adrian wander across to where Mrs Emery was still seated with the other VIPs.

A waiter crossed my field of vision. He was bent over our table, gathering dirty plates onto a tray. With a shock of adrenaline, I recognised those strong shoulders. And that cute arse.

Jake. Of course he would be here, if what I feared was

true—despite the fact that he could hardly pick a more dangerous place for a fireshaper if he tried. I noticed he stuck to the edges of the room, and kept his back to Mrs Emery as much as possible.

He straightened and turned away, heading for the kitchens with a purposeful stride. I steeled myself for another round of accusations. My heart had started to race the minute I recognised him. I just hoped nobody else did; he'd said he'd seen Mrs Emery before. Would she know him again? I couldn't help worrying, just a little—he was well and truly outnumbered here. The shit would really hit the fan if these people discovered one of the hated shapers lurking in their midst.

I made another slow circuit of the dance floor, my mind whirling faster than my body. He hadn't even looked at me, but he must know I was here. When we came around to that side of the dance floor again, I looked for Mrs Emery, but her table was now empty. There was no sign of Jake, nor of Adrian. Glancing around, I couldn't see Bruno or Irene either. Where had they all gone? Fear clenched at my insides. Had Jake been caught?

"Excuse me," I said to Matt. "I need to visit the ladies'."

"No problem," he said, though I felt his eyes on me all the way across the room. Had he been given the job of keeping me out of the way while the others all went and did whatever they were doing to create the new Zephyrs? If only that was all they were doing. Where was Jake?

I hurried along the hallway. A couple of waiters passed me, but neither of them were Jake. There was no sign of any scowling fireshapers lurking. I found an office, and a door that opened into a cavernous garage, big enough for half a dozen cars. I found the bathroom, too, and swinging doors that didn't disguise the busy clattering sounds of the kitchen. But I didn't find Mrs Emery and her cohort.

Jake had said she was trouble. As the minutes ticked by with no sign of any of them, my stomach knotted tighter and tighter. Where was he? There'd been something not quite right about Mrs Emery from the moment I met her— I shivered at the memory of her creepy fingers brushing across my tattoo. But I hadn't wanted to believe it, hadn't wanted to believe Jake when he'd insisted she was bad news, too caught up in my dream of being one big, happy family with all the other Aristaeans. Now Jake was missing, and I had to find him.

They'd probably gone upstairs. I hesitated at the foot of the sweeping staircase. I supposed I could say I was looking for the bathroom if anyone found me poking around up there. Magnificent floor-to-ceiling bookcases lined the hallway beyond the staircase. As I put my foot on the first step, I noticed that one of those bookcases was out of alignment. One side of it jutted out from its neighbour.

Now *that* looked more promising than checking out a bunch of bedrooms. I hurried over and gave that side of the bookcase an experimental tug. It was heavy, but it moved. Now we were talking. Nothing warmed the cockles of a thief's heart like a good old-fashioned hidden door.

My excitement was short-lived. The door chose that moment to swing open, nearly taking me out in the process. A man whose hulking presence screamed "bodyguard" stepped through and shut the door behind him. He regarded me with deep suspicion.

"Can I help you, miss?"

"I was … just looking for the bathroom."

"Down the hallway on the right."

"Thanks."

He took up a position in front of the door as I slunk away. When I looked back, he was still there, guarding a wall of books and watching me. Looked like I wouldn't be getting past him any time soon.

I slipped into the bathroom and locked the door behind me. That was okay. There were more ways to kill a cat than drowning it in cream.

10

I sent my awareness out through the house, past the guard and the door he guarded, looking for a bright spark of animal life to guide me. Not surprisingly for such a well-staffed and clean establishment, there weren't many options, but I found a spider hanging in a dark corner beyond the bookcase door. Through its eyes I saw a staircase descending. It was only a little spider, not the sort to send scurrying down the stairs, so I moved on, hoping to find something to show me a little more of what lay below the public areas of the house.

A moth fluttered close to a naked light bulb in a dim room below my feet. I forced it away from its single-minded suicide mission and saw a group of people passing beneath it. One of them could have been Mrs Emery, though it was hard to tell through the moth's eyes. A man broke away from the group and opened a door I hadn't noticed, spilling more light into the room. I sent the moth in fluttering pursuit and found myself outside in the lamplit night. Damn. The man did nothing more interesting than take up an unobtrusive guard outside the door, so I set the moth free and searched for another set of eyes back inside the dark spaces under the house.

Unfortunately, I came up empty-handed. But I was more determined than ever to find out what was going on down there. The little I had seen looked like a wine cellar, which made sense for a place that had been a winery before it became a rich woman's country estate, and I'd had the sense of a large space. Though I guess, to a moth, anything would seem large. I needed to see for myself.

I left the bathroom and wandered back to the original room where we'd had pre-dinner drinks, past my suspicious friend at the bookcase door. From there, I let myself out onto the terrace. It was cold outside, and goose bumps rose on my bare arms, but I took the steps down from the terrace as if it were the perfect night to wander around admiring the lamplit gardens.

They were certainly pretty, even in the dark. There were fairy lights in the trees here, too, and the lake at the bottom of the little hill reflected the moon in its still waters. I followed a gravel path that sloped gently down toward the lake as it curved around the back of the house.

About halfway along the house, I found what I was

looking for. A terraced garden jutted out above, and the drop down to the next level was a good three metres. Built into the side of that drop was a heavy wooden door, partly concealed by shrubbery. Most people would probably have wandered right past, since it was in a dark area away from the lamp posts that lit the rest of the garden. In the lights blazing from the house above, I could make out the figure of the man standing quietly in the shadows by the door.

Now what? I wasn't dressed for business, and had no knives on me. Not that I was in the habit of cutting random strangers just for the crime of being in my way, but the knives made me feel safer. I thought I could make out the bulge of a gun under his jacket. What were they doing in there that they needed an armed guard on the door?

The guard must have seen me, so I turned as if I was admiring the lake below, keeping him in my peripheral vision. Two possums scampered in the trees by the lake; perhaps I could use them to distract the guard long enough to slip past him.

A shadow moved on the terraced garden above the guard, a man's figure silhouetted against the lights from the house.

Jake again.

Thank God—he hadn't been caught. My heart did a little flip of relief. But he obviously had no experience at sneaking up on people. If he didn't stop rustling around up there, the guard would be waiting for him with gun at the ready, and he *would* be caught. Damn. I couldn't let that happen. Plastering a smile on my face, I turned on my heel and walked back toward the guard.

"Hey there! I almost didn't see you back there in the dark. Have you got a light?"

I didn't have a cigarette, which would shortly become super embarrassing, if Jake didn't follow through. The guard stepped forward, digging obligingly into his trouser pocket, and I moved smartly out of the way as Jake leapt and felled him with a blow to the head.

We stood over the guard's body, staring at each other. Jake was shaking out his fist and breathing hard, but I didn't flatter myself that had anything to do with me.

"You distracted him for me."

"You seemed like you needed a hand."

He still wore his waiter's suit, and he took his time adjusting the jacket, brushing off leaves and bits of twig. Then he crouched down and rifled through the unconscious man's pockets, emerging with a set of keys.

"What are you doing out here?" Well, at least we hadn't progressed straight to accusations about the ring. "Why aren't you inside with your new friends?"

"I'm not sure if they're really my friends."

"Really? You're not friends with a bunch of One World killers? You amaze me. I thought that was just your kind of crowd." The savagery in his voice gave me chills. Some of my delight at finding him safe began to fade.

"They're not killers," I said, but the objection didn't carry as much force as it might have done a few days ago. Things were definitely not adding up around here. Or rather, they were adding up to something I didn't want to face. "But something strange is going on. Somehow, these people are giving themselves powers."

He gave me a disgusted look, then flipped the guard's jacket open to reveal that he did indeed carry a gun. Jake took the gun out and pinched the end of the barrel in his fingers. The opening melted shut like putty. Phew. For a minute there, he'd looked as though he'd like to use it on me.

He replaced the now useless gun in its holster and dragged the guy further into the bushes, where no one passing by would be able to see him. "*Somehow* they're giving themselves powers?" His voice was laden with bitterness. "I'll tell you how—they're shadow shapers. Haven't you listened to anything Alberto and I have been telling you? They're murdering gods and stealing their powers for themselves."

Murdering gods? I'd had my suspicions, but man, it sucked to be proven right. I stared at his rigid back as he unlocked the door. What the hell had I got myself into?

"But *how*? How do you murder a god?"

134

"Do I *look* like a shadow shaper? I'm not up on the details. I just know they need both the god and his avatar. Like that ring you insist you know nothing about. Once they have that, it's goodbye god, hello new shadow shapers. And if we don't stop them soon, it'll be goodbye fireshapers and watershapers and every other elemental shaper as well. Once all the gods are dead, our powers die too."

"Then why did Anders want the bloody ring so much? You said he was working with the shadow shapers. Why would a fireshaper be in league with these people if helping them would destroy his own power?"

His face twisted into a snarl. "Who knows why a man like that does the things he does? Most likely, he figured that if he got the ring he could become a shadow shaper too. He was never much of a fireshaper. Perhaps he thought it was inevitable that the shadow shapers would succeed in killing all the gods, and he wanted to ensure he'd still have *some* kind of power once the dust settled."

He started to close the door on me, and I leapt forward. "Wait! Jake, who is Aristaeus? Do you know?"

He stared at me, his face unreadable. "Aristaeus was the god of animal husbandry, among other things. He was also the deity who watched over the harvest of fruit trees. Gardeners and beekeepers prayed to him. He was killed by the shadow shapers a year ago."

Beekeepers? Dear God.

"Adrian …" Adrian had power over bees. He thought I did, too, which made me an Aristaean like him. But there weren't many of us, Matt had said, because Aristaeus wasn't very powerful. Now I understood. I closed the door behind us, and leaned back against it for a moment. "Adrian is an Aristaean."

Adrian was a shadow shaper. They probably all were. The people Jake had been hunting, that he hated more than anything else—because they were murderers, killing the gods he loved and stealing their power. Was I one of them?

Bile rose in my throat. No, it was impossible. I wasn't a killer!

But I *was* a thief. What bigger theft could there be than stealing their own power from the gods? Doubt assailed me. My memory was all kinds of screwy, and I didn't know where my power had come from. Could I have forgotten something like this?

It was darker in the cellar than it had been in the garden outside. The single light bulb that my moth had shown me was very dim, and barely illuminated a little circular patch beneath it. Its light didn't reach into the corners at all, and Jake's face was in shadow. I sagged against the door, staring at him while a sick feeling churned in my gut.

"So now you care?" he asked, his tone laden with suspicion. "That's a rather sudden change of heart, isn't it?"

"What about Cybele? Who is that?" Might as well know it all.

"A nature goddess. A *former* nature goddess."

And I was betting she'd had some power to control birds or animals, hence Adrian's assumption when I'd attacked him with the owl. The evidence that I was associated with these murderers was stacking up, but my heart refused to accept it.

"What are you going to do?" I asked.

It was cold in here, and had the dank, underground smell of earth. Opposite was the stairway that led up to the bookcase door. On either side, a large stone archway opened into darkness. If the way had been lit before, it wasn't any more. I wasn't even sure which way Mrs Emery's party had gone. I peered into the darkness beyond the arches, my mind reeling.

Okay, think about this calmly for a minute. My memory was playing tricks on me, but I'd have to be a completely different kind of person to associate with coldblooded killers like these. I just couldn't believe I was one of them. "Can I help you?"

"Why would you help now? You've got this suspicious ability to mess with animals. You've already given them Apollo's ring. Oh, no, that's right—you swear you haven't seen it. How can I trust you to help me rescue him?" The bitterness was back, even stronger than before. "Every time

I finally decide you're on my side, you do something else that makes me doubt you again. Half the time I want to kiss you, and the other half I want to kill you." He loomed over me in the dark, fists clenched. Looked like the killing half was winning again. "We'll probably get in there and you'll hand me over to your new boyfriend. I should knock you out and leave you out there with the other guy."

Ouch. That stung, even though I'd brought it on myself by stealing the ring and running. He was right; he shouldn't trust me, though I hadn't done what he accused me of. But I could see why he thought so, when even *I* wondered if I was actually one of these people. Maybe I didn't deserve anyone's trust. But I wished I had his.

Why did his good opinion matter? Because he was ... my friend? The idea of being friends with a shaper would have made me laugh only a week ago. Maybe more than a friend? Best not to think too hard about that. Whatever he was, he was trying to save his god, which all seemed too big and scary to be any of my business, but here I was, and he needed help. And I didn't approve of people being murdered for their power, gods or not. In the end, that was enough to convince me that, whatever I was, I wasn't a shadow shaper.

But most of all, I wanted him to look at me with that old speculative twinkle in his eyes again, not this hostility and suspicion.

I came to a decision on the spot. Syl would be rolling her eyes if she was here; she was always complaining about me acting impulsively. But I *had* considered doing it before, and now I was sure it was right.

I pulled the ring off my finger, ignoring the whisper that felt like a protest, and offered it to him. "Here. Have it back if it means so much to you."

He stared down at the plain gold band lying in my palm, confusion on his face. Oops. I pushed my awareness at the ring. *Come on, you're going to have to convince him.*

I felt a tickle in my mind, then the ring shimmered in my hand and resumed its original form of the golden sun with its radiating rays.

Jake flinched, then gave me a suspicious frown. "How did you do that?"

"It wasn't me," I said truthfully—I hoped. At least, it hadn't *felt* like something I'd done. "The ring can change itself."

Tentatively, he reached out and took it. I shivered at the brush of his fingers on the sensitive skin of my palm, suddenly aware how close he stood in the darkness. He held the ring up to the hanging bulb's dim light, turning it this way and that, as if to convince himself it was real.

Evidently satisfied, he thrust it into an inside pocket of his jacket and turned his attention back to me. His expression was friendlier, if still wary. His hand came up to cup my face, and he sighed. "You are the most infuriating woman I have ever met."

Yay, me? I closed my eyes, breathing in the familiar, slightly smoky scent of him. His thumb stroked my cheek and I shivered, leaning into his touch.

"Thank you," he added. His lips brushed mine and my eyes flew open to find him smiling down at me. "One of these days, when people aren't trying to kill us, maybe I'll have a chance to do that properly."

Then he strode off into the darkness, leaving me gaping after him. Damn the man.

When he realised I wasn't following, he paused under the left-hand arch. "You coming?"

Not yet, Fire Boy, but maybe soon. I followed him, more than a little distracted by the promise of that future. It was almost embarrassing how much I liked the idea of being thoroughly kissed by him. At least he couldn't see my face flaming in the dark.

11

The cellar smelled of old dirt and spilled wine; a kind of sour mix of both. It wasn't precisely unpleasant, but it was strong. Syl would hate it here—shifters had such sensitive noses.

Beneath our feet, the floor was packed earth and deathly cold. Already, I could feel the chill creeping up my bare legs. Of course, a sleeveless cocktail dress wouldn't have been my first choice for exploring dangerous new situations, but I'd dressed for a party, not a rescue mission.

Jake moved slowly until our eyes grew more accustomed to the low light levels, picking his way across the uneven floor. Huge barrels and mysterious pieces of abandoned winemaking equipment were stacked up in haphazard arrangements against the walls, and sprawling out into the centre of the large open area we moved through. A number of stone archways broke up the space into unknowable little nooks and crannies. There could have been enemies lurking anywhere, and my skin crawled with apprehension. I was used to hunting at night, but something about this set-up had me spooked.

After nerve-wracking moments of this creeping progress, we arrived at a heavy wooden door barring our way. I cast my awareness beyond the door, searching for a spider, a bug—anything—to give me a glimpse of what lay beyond, but no little sparks of life greeted me. These cellars were emptier of animal life than the most arid desert.

"How do you know that Apollo's here?" I whispered.

His eyes glittered strangely in the dim light as he looked at me. "To be honest, I thought that's why you'd come here. I was afraid you were one of them, and you were bringing them Apollo's ring, so I followed you from Berkley's Bay. But he must be here if that Emery woman is. She likes to keep him close."

He laid his hand on his jacket for a moment, as if to assure himself that the ring was still safe in his pocket, then he turned the handle and eased the door open by degrees. Hints of sound drifted out, the kind of sounds made by a large group of people waiting in silence for something: the scuff of a foot against the earthen floor, the rustle of someone's clothing as they moved, a sigh here, a whisper there. As he slipped through the doorway, I tensed for a shout of discovery, but when I joined him I found another darkened room, empty of anything but more wine barrels.

But through one of the archways leading off from this new room was a much bigger space, and here, we finally found the people. We sank down behind the cover of a pile of barrels and peeked into the next room.

Mrs Emery was there, and Adrian next to her, as well as perhaps thirty others, though from my narrow vantage point in the gap between two barrels, I couldn't be sure of numbers. A woman who looked like Irene had her back to me, though I couldn't see Bruno. They all stood in a loose circle around a giant stone table that had iron rings sunk into its surface at each corner. The thing practically screamed "altar". The scene was lit only by the light of flickering torches shoved into brackets on the walls. How bizarre. What was wrong with good old electric lighting? Maybe they were trying for a theatrical effect with the flames and the dancing shadows they cast.

As we watched, a ripple ran through the gathering at the sound of footsteps approaching. Two burly men emerged from a side passage, with another man between them, struggling in their grip. The watchers stirred and shifted and murmured to their neighbours as this man was dragged toward the central altar.

Jake hissed. I glanced at him, but his eyes were glued to the scene unfolding on the other side of the archway. The man was only young, dressed in jeans and tatty sneakers.

He wore no shirt, and his skinny frame was pasty white, as if he'd been imprisoned in the dark for a long time. Lank hair hung over his face, and the rest of him wasn't too clean either. Around his neck, he wore the strangest piece of jewellery, for want of a better name—like one of those torcs ancient kings used to wear, or maybe a slave collar, though it was decorated with far too many pretty swirls and rune-like markings to be a slave collar. It shone a dull silver, but it was beautiful, and it seemed decidedly out of place on its somewhat scruffy wearer.

I leaned closer to Jake. "Is that Apollo?" I whispered.

If this was the legendary sun god, I had to admit I was a bit disappointed. But then, Hades had disguised himself as the ultimate vampire. I was guessing that gods could take on any form they pleased.

"No. They don't have the ring. They won't kill him until they have that."

"Then who is it?"

"No idea. It could be anyone."

"Adrian said they were making Zephyrs tonight."

"Zeus's balls. Then it's Zephyrus. God of the west wind."

Zephyrus was fighting every step of the way, jerking and kicking against his captors as if he knew what was in store for him in that torchlit room. But they forced him right up to the altar, where Adrian waited with handcuffs ready.

"We have to stop this," Jake muttered, rising from his crouch. "We have to save him."

"It's too risky. You're here to save Apollo." Now I sounded like the ever-pragmatic Syl, but I didn't think we were going to get more than one shot at this. I caught at his arm; the muscles were tense, ready for action. "We can search for him while everyone's distracted with this guy."

He glared down at me. "He's not just some guy. That's a *god*. Do you want every airshaper in the world to wake up tomorrow weaker than when they went to bed? Every god that dies weakens all of us. I can't stand by and do nothing while they slaughter him. Between us, we can take them."

I sighed, and rose to stand beside him. Alrighty then. Time for a desperate mission with the odds stacked against us. My favourite sort. Now I wished we'd taken that guard's gun instead of disabling it and leaving it behind. I felt naked with no weapons and no animals to call to my aid. "I'm afraid I'm not going to be much help."

"You've got powers."

I spread my arms. "Do you see any animals here?"

Suspicion was back in his eyes. "How convenient. But it doesn't matter. If I take that Emery bitch out first, the rest will crumble." His hand crept to his throat for a moment. "I haven't got one of her collars on now. Let's see how she likes it when I can fight back."

I swallowed the hurt of his renewed suspicion. Clearly,

I'd have to earn back his trust. I just hoped he was powerful enough to take out a room full of shadow shapers, because he wasn't going to get much help from me. Though, as I watched them force the unfortunate god up onto the altar and Adrian cuff his right wrist to the first iron ring, I could think of one person I'd happily take out with a well-placed kick to the gonads. To think I'd ever thought Adrian seemed like a decent guy. I was such a crappy judge of men.

Jake leapt out into full view, though only a couple of people noticed him. The others were intent on the drama taking place in their midst. They noticed him all right, though, when two bolts of flame shot from his hands and engulfed the men manhandling Zephyrus between them. As they fell, screaming, Adrian leapt back with a very unmanly shriek, and the room devolved into chaos.

Some fled down the passageway from which the god and his guards had emerged; others tried to take cover behind the ever-present barrels, or fled from the burning, writhing men. In the centre of the madness, Zephyrus knelt up on the stone altar, tugging futilely at the one handcuff that held him prisoner, his face alight with hope. Unfortunately, Mrs Emery sheltered behind him, and Jake couldn't firebomb her for fear of hitting him.

Jake stalked forward like a fiery avenging angel and I followed, intent on Adrian. First the gonads, and then I'd search him for the key to that handcuff. The smell of cooking

146

flesh made me gag, but I avoided looking at the burning men and focused on the job at hand instead. They'd known what they were doing. They didn't deserve my pity.

For a moment, it seemed Jake had prevailed as simply as that. These people were all supposed to have powers of their own, but none of them seemed to remember that in the shock of the moment—or maybe, like Adrian, they only had power over bees or other tricks that would be no use in a firefight. Then Mrs Emery reached out and snatched the second handcuff from Adrian's hand.

She brought it down so hard against Zephyrus's temple that he dropped like a stone and lay crumpled on the altar. Then, cool as if flames weren't whipping past her head as Jake sprayed the room with fire, she pulled something from her pocket and applied it to the back of the strange collar Zephyrus wore. A key? I was guessing it must be as the collar opened, hinged at the front.

Everything happened so quickly. I was halfway across the room. Jake was lashing people with tendrils of fire from the torches burning on the walls. And Mrs Emery, with deadly aim, hurled the collar straight at him.

There must have been magic involved. The thing homed in on Jake as if he were a beacon and snapped shut around his neck. He didn't even see it coming until the last second, too late to do anything about it. His flames died instantly, snuffed out as if they'd never been.

His hands flew to the thing around his neck, his face a picture of horror.

Mrs Emery smirked, and gestured to the men at her side. "You can take them now. He can't access his power anymore."

My mind raced. I hadn't actually moved against any of them. Perhaps I could still salvage something from this debacle.

As the men surrounded Jake, I stepped forward, a confident smile plastered on my face. "I hope you like the present I brought you," I said to Mrs Emery.

She stopped, and one eyebrow lifted as she examined me. "*You* brought him here?"

"Lured him here, would be a better way of putting it."

It was just as well she'd cut off Jake's powers, because I would have been a pile of charcoal if he'd had access to them at that moment. The look he gave me burned with a naked hatred that did more to convince Mrs Emery than any story I could have spun.

"I knew there was something special about you. You're that friend of Adrian's, aren't you?" She glanced at Adrian. He would never know how close his gonads had come to annihilation. *One day*, I promised myself.

"Yes," he said, though he looked unsure about being associated with me. If I had my way, it would certainly turn out to be a career-limiting move.

"And how did you come to know this fireshaper well enough to lure him here?" Mrs Emery completely ignored the god slumped on the altar next to her, the blackened bodies on the floor, even the other people milling uncertainly in the room. Her tone was as cool as if we were upstairs at the gala still, chatting over champagne and canapés. My dislike of this woman was growing by the minute, but I hid it with another smile.

"I'm an Aristaean," I said, though even pretending it was true made me sick. "I've been living in the shaper territories undercover."

All the fight had gone out of Jake once the collar had snapped shut around his neck. He stared at the floor, not even struggling as one of the men cuffed his hands behind his back. I didn't look at him—I couldn't bear to see the hatred in his eyes again. I longed to comfort him, but I had a part to play.

"Well done," she said to me, then jerked her head at one of the men, who began to pat Jake down.

Oh, shit. My mouth went dry. *Now* Jake struggled, but it was too late. My knees trembled as the man drew forth the ring from Jake's inner pocket and held it out for Mrs Emery's inspection.

Her eyes gleamed as she held out an imperious hand. "A fireshaper *and* a bonus," she breathed as her fingers closed around the ring. "I like you more and more. What was your name again?"

"Lexi Jardine." My heart was hammering so loudly I wouldn't have been surprised if she could hear it way over the other side of the room. Would they kill Apollo now? They had the ring; there was nothing stopping them any more. *Why* had I given it to Jake? It would have been safe on my finger with no one the wiser. God, I was a fool.

"Come in, Lexi." She spread her arms wide in welcome. "Share with us the bounty of one united world, ruled by humans, for humans. Adrian," she added, in a much snappier tone, "fetch another collar."

Adrian scurried away like a dog doing its master's bidding and returned with another of the silver, rune-covered collars. Now that I knew what they could do, it no longer looked so pretty. It also looked remarkably similar to the ornamental cuff around Mrs Emery's own wrist; I figured it gave her some kind of control of the collars. She snapped the new one closed around Zephyrus's neck with almost a look of boredom. The god hadn't moved; I couldn't tell whether he was unconscious or dead.

Adrian and another man stretched him out, moving his limbs as if he were a marionette, and secured him to the altar. Presumably he was alive, then. No point chaining a dead body. A couple of other men dragged the charred bodies of Jake's victims away, while everyone tried to ignore the shaper in their midst, standing with his head hanging in despair.

I wished I could communicate with him mind to mind, reassure him that I was on his side, at least, even if there wasn't much else reassuring to say about our situation. Had Mrs Emery only collared Jake to control him, or did she mean to kill him too? My stomach roiled with nerves as I waited for whatever would happen next.

I didn't have to wait long. At a signal from Mrs Emery, another woman brought forward a tiny flute on a green velvet cushion. It looked like something that would normally be dangling off a keyring, but from the reverent hush that greeted its appearance, I was guessing it was a touch more important than that.

The woman stopped beside Adrian, and he lifted the little charm from the cushion and laid it on the unconscious god's chest. I glanced across at Jake, but he refused to raise his head. Maybe that was a good idea—I had a bad feeling about what was coming next, but I felt compelled to watch the drama play out in all its appalling detail. If I couldn't save the poor bastard, at least I could bear witness to his death.

Sure enough, another cushion bearer appeared at Adrian's side, and this one bore a knife. Not a slim, quiet knife like my throwing knives—and how I wished I had them now; I'd put one through that bitch Emery's heart—

but a big, ostentatious dagger. Its hilt was inlaid with rubies and engraved with all kinds of swirling patterns, and the gleaming blade was long, with a slight curve on it. Adrian glanced at Mrs Emery and she gave him an encouraging nod.

With two hands, Adrian lifted the dagger from its cushion and held it aloft so that everyone could see it. The blade glittered red in the flickering torchlight, as if it had already tasted blood.

"May this new power, shared among us, herald a new age of hope for humanity. May those gathered here to receive it wield this power always for the good of the people they guard."

And with no more ceremony than that, he slashed the god's throat in one vicious movement. I flinched. It was so sudden and shocking. Bright red blood sprayed the cushion-bearer beside him: she flinched, too, though she tried to pretend she hadn't, valiantly ignoring the blood that dripped down her arm and stained her cocktail dress.

No one else seemed perturbed by the brief violence. They all watched the god still, as if expecting something more to happen. Like vultures circling the dying, their faces held hunger and greed. Adrian's eyes gleamed with anticipation, and the whole room seemed to be holding its breath.

A golden glow began to form around the little silver flute

where it lay on the god's chest, now spattered with his lifeblood. For a moment, it shone so brightly it was hard to look at, but it quickly faded away again, leaving the flute plain silver as before.

The people around me let out a collective breath. Evidently some important part of their gruesome ritual had just occurred. Had the god's life force or soul just passed into the flute? His power? Whatever it was, it seemed to make the watchers happy. They shifted and rustled as if the best was yet to come.

Mrs Emery took the bloody flute and lay it on the stone altar by the dead god's side. Moving it out of the way for the next part of the ceremony, apparently. Adrian stepped closer, knife still clutched firmly in his hand.

He had his back to me, so I didn't see what he did, but it soon became obvious. Triumphantly, he raised a dark red hunk of meat above his head, rivulets of blood running down from both bloodied hands.

It was the god's heart.

It wasn't still beating, or anything crazy like that; it was just a piece of meat. The scent of fresh blood filled the room and my stomach protested the butchery. I swallowed hard, managing to hold it together as he paraded the heart like a goddamn trophy.

And then things got really sicko. Adrian sliced a piece off the heart and popped it into his mouth. I nearly lost my dinner then. Even Jake made a sound of protest. Adrian moved around the room, offering a piece of heart to everyone present.

When he got to me, he looked a question back at Mrs Emery. She hadn't joined in the gruesome feast. She shook her head.

"Not for you, dear." Well, that suited me just fine. Cannibalism really wasn't my thing. "I have a much greater reward in mind for you."

Oh, goody. I could hardly wait. Adrian continued around the circle until he arrived back at the starting point. Some of the diners looked a little green as they choked down the raw flesh, but everyone seemed determined.

When everyone had eaten, Adrian washed his hands in a silver bowl brought to him by Irene. He dried them on a snow-white towel, leaving pinkish smears across the fabric. So much blood everywhere. It had pooled underneath the victim's body and crept across to the edge of the altar. Now it dripped steadily onto the floor, the tiny sound of each drop hitting the packed earth like an accusation.

Now Mrs Emery herself brought out a massive hammer. It looked like something you could take into battle—it had been designed to destroy rather than build. It also had many swirling designs etched into its head, and rubies glittered on the long shaft like drops of blood. It must have weighed a ton, but Mrs Emery handled it easily.

She lined up the huge head over the tiny silver flute, then took a massive backswing. With a grunt of effort, she brought the hammer crashing down, and the flute broke into several pieces, crushed beneath the hammer's great weight.

A golden light burst from the broken flute, washing out through the room. It flared briefly over the body of every person who'd eaten of the heart, so for a moment, they all shone like golden statues. Then it faded away, sinking into their skin.

An awed silence filled the room. I felt sick. This was how it was done, then. Kill a god and wait until all his power had entered his avatar, then eat his heart and destroy the avatar. Stand back and watch the power rush out to fill the gathered thieves and murderers. Rinse and repeat. This was how you created shadow shapers.

Across the room, I met Irene's gaze. She looked like a woman who'd just had the very best sex of her life. Her tongue flicked out and licked at a smear of blood on her face. The same look of smug self-satisfaction was reflected all around the room.

These people were rotten to the core. I looked at the lone shaper in their midst, symbol of everything I had ever hated, and wondered how I could have been so wrong. Jake was here to save, not destroy, and he was worth more than all these sick monsters put together. My heart damn near broke at the anguish on his face. It was time to stop fighting my attraction to him, just because he was a shaper. What we were didn't define us, only what we did.

Right then and there, I changed sides. If these were the humans, I wanted nothing to do with them. From now on, I was on Team Shaper.

12

They hustled Jake away down the corridor they'd brought Zephyrus from, and the rest of us went back upstairs to the public parts of the house, the new shadow shapers still buzzing with excitement. They probably could have partied all night, but Mrs Emery shooed them out the door, saying she had a long drive ahead of her in the morning.

I hovered next to Adrian, feeling time slipping away from me. I was so tired I was reeling on my feet, and there wasn't a lot of the night left. Now they had Apollo's avatar, it surely wouldn't be long before Apollo himself would be stretched out on that altar, which meant I had to come up with a plan to free Jake pretty damn fast. I had no illusions that my favourite fireshaper would outlive the god he worshipped.

"What's going to happen to the fireshaper?" I asked.

Adrian smiled at me. "You did so well with him. I understand your impatience, but you'll have to wait until Apollo arrives tomorrow."

I smiled back, though it was a struggle. He still had Zephyrus's blood crusted in the corner of his mouth, and I would rather have shed some blood myself than smiled at such a man. "He's not here?" So much for Jake's theory that Apollo would be wherever Mrs Emery was.

"No. Mrs Emery's had him hidden away somewhere so secret not even Mike Newton knows where it is. It's a security thing, in case the fireshapers tried another rescue."

Mrs Emery joined us. "Are you all right, Lexi? You look exhausted."

"It's been a busy few days."

She patted me on the arm. "We must get you a bed. This house is full of empty rooms."

"I'd love to stay, but my cat's back at the motel."

"You're staying in a motel? But that's ridiculous. You've done such a wonderful thing, bringing me that ring. I insist you stay here. It will give the servants something to do," she added, with majestic disregard for her servants' workload. "And really, after living undercover in the shaper cities, you deserve spoiling. You must tell me all about your adventures when I get back. Adrian can look after you in the meantime. Adrian, don't let her out of your sight. I expect you to be at her beck and call. Dear Lexi deserves every comfort."

Clearly, she was a woman used to having her word treated as law, because she strode off, trailed by a bevy of admirers and bodyguards, before I could object. In her mind, the subject was settled. Adrian obviously didn't get a say.

"But I can't just leave my cat," I said to Adrian. We were alone now in the spacious foyer, except for the odd servant hurrying past on clean-up duties. They wouldn't be getting to bed any time soon, not that anyone seemed to care. "She's got no food."

"Why do you have a *cat*?" He sounded as revolted as if I'd announced I'd just taken a dump on the middle of his bed.

"It was important to blend in in the shaper territories. Having a pet made them trust me."

"Yes, but now you're back ..."

I shrugged, as if to say, *yeah, it's weird, but what can you do?* "I became attached to her."

"Well, I guess I could take you to pick her up tomorrow," he said doubtfully.

"Couldn't we go tonight?" My schedule for tomorrow was already jam-packed with trying to rescue a certain fireshaper.

He still looked uncomfortable with the idea, but Mrs Emery's words about being at my beck and call had obviously had an effect. "I'll have to talk to the staff about accommodating the animal here."

"Oh, she'll be no problem. She can just sleep on my bed like she usually does."

Revulsion flickered across his features, but he agreed, and we went out to his car once he'd alerted the staff to the imminent arrival of "the animal". As if she were some kind of rabid beast. If I wasn't so heartsore, I could have laughed at the idea.

Adrian's car was the last left on the grass beside the driveway. It gleamed dully silver under the lamplight, reminding me uncomfortably of the colour of the collar around the dead god's neck—and now around Jake's. Presumably Apollo, wherever he was, wore one too.

Once we were under way, sliding silently down the now-deserted roads, Adrian's mood picked up again. I suppose having a new power zipping around your bloodstream could do that to a person, as long as the coldblooded murder that preceded the acquisition didn't trouble the conscience too much. From what I'd seen of the shadow shapers so far, none of them seemed to *have* consciences.

"I couldn't believe it when the two of you appeared out of the dark like that," he said, lost in fond reminiscence.

Honestly, killing was too good for these people. In the old days, the gods had had the right idea—look at poor old Prometheus, having his liver snacked on by that eagle every day for all eternity. But why hadn't the gods swatted them down to size already? I needed to talk to Hades about that.

He'd said the gods didn't work together well, too scared of the shadow shapers—but how had the shadow shapers become such a threat? Where had they come from, with their controlling collars? And how did they get one of those collars onto a god in the first place? There was still a lot I didn't understand.

"I doubted you then, I have to admit," Adrian continued. "I thought we were done for when the shaper started tossing fire around. But good old Mrs E always thinks on her feet—you should see her at the negotiating table. And then you were behind it all along." His glance was full of admiration. "That moment when Charles pulled out the ring—sheer perfection. Do you know how long we've been searching for that thing?"

"Quite a while?" I guessed.

He threw me a boyish smile, which, frankly, made me queasy now I'd seen his knifework. Psychopaths really weren't my thing. "But of course you'd know. That's probably why you went into the shaper territories in the first place, isn't it?"

I made a non-committal noise.

"Oh, it's all right, you don't have to tell me the details. I'm sure it's all very hush-hush. Rather you than me—I couldn't stand to live among those abominations. It would make me sick, having to treat them like real humans."

"It was pretty tough," I agreed. Jake certainly had been

annoying at times. I shifted uncomfortably in my seat as anxiety gnawed at me. Maybe I'd wished him in hell once or twice, but not like this. Besides which, my sentiments about shapers had undergone a radical change since I'd met him. If someone had offered to slaughter Erik Anders, I would have cheered them on, but I'd come to understand that shapers weren't all like him. *Jake* wasn't like him. I had to save him, but I didn't know how, and barely-concealed panic was eating me up inside.

"It was a nice touch, bringing the shaper as well as the avatar. They had him once before, in Bourneville. Caught him trying to free Apollo. I heard they beat him almost to death, but the bastard still managed to escape with Apollo's ring. I think Mrs E will be almost as pleased to finish him off as she will to finally be done with Apollo." He turned off the freeway, following the signs for Newport City Centre. "It's been a constant stress, worrying that there will be another attempt to free the god. Those damn fireshapers are persistent. That's why she's kept his location secret, and kept moving him around."

For a moment, remembering those terrible whipping scars on Jake's back, I was too angry to speak. *I heard they beat him almost to death.* How casually he spoke of it, as if Jake's life meant nothing. To think I'd thought the shapers were arrogant!

"But surely, with those collars, there's not much chance

of escape." I gritted my teeth and forced myself to keep my tone light and conversational. My brain was really too tired for these mental gymnastics—trying to find out information while still trying to sound like I knew what I was talking about. And the toughest part was resisting the urge to administer a good beating myself. I'd love nothing more than to wipe that smug look off his face. But I had to stick it out for Jake's sake.

"Well, she's certainly more careful with the key to the collars since the fireshaper escaped." He laughed knowingly. "She's not likely to be pickpocketed again! It's always locked in the safe now unless she's actually using it."

"I wonder she didn't just kill Apollo if she was so worried, and give up on the ring."

He gave me an odd look. "And lose all that power? If gods didn't keep so much of their strength in their avatars, sure. Maybe in the old days, when they weren't trying to pass as human by hiding their power—but now? If all the power's in the avatar so they can look human, and you don't have the avatar when you kill them—well, the shapers you'd create would be very weak shadows indeed. It almost wouldn't be worth doing at all. And he's the *sun god*. It would be criminal to waste all that power."

"True." Well, that explained all the fuss over the ring. "I guess it's all over now, so she won't have to worry any more."

"Not after tomorrow night," he agreed.

I felt sick—I had so little time. "It's all happening so fast."

"No point waiting, is there? I think we've waited long enough. Mrs E will head off at first light to retrieve Apollo, and we'll have to wait for a couple of the bigwigs from Bourneville to fly in, but we should be ready to go by nightfall. By this time tomorrow, we'll both be Apollonians. Has a nice ring to it, doesn't it?"

"Mmm." I was starting to recognise the dark streets we were passing through. We weren't far now from the motel. "How many shadows have we created now? Do you know?" That could be useful information. And how many of them would I have to go through to get to Jake?

"I'm sure Mrs E's got a list, but I couldn't say for sure. I know they've done a few harvests in Bourneville and a couple of other places, as well as the ones we've done here. Plus, we have quite a few multis, like you and I." He winked. "Gotta make sure the top people are rewarded, right?"

"Right." Everyone was equal, but some were more equal than others. When had humans ever been any different? They bitched and moaned about the shapers, and how unfair it was that they could use their powers to lord it over the powerless, but the minute they got their hands on any kind of advantage, they began building their own hierarchies of haves and have-nots. "But just at a rough guess? What would you say?"

He shrugged. "Five hundred? I don't know. As I say, I'm not sure what they've been up to in the other cities. Maybe as many as a thousand. Bruno might have a better idea."

"Maybe I'll ask him tomorrow, then, if he's there."

"Oh, he'll be there all right. Wouldn't miss it for the world."

He pulled up outside my motel. Half the letters in its neon sign had gone out, adding to the rundown air created by the weeds growing through the cracks in the concrete driveway, and the few scabrous twigs sticking out of the plant pot by the office door.

"You'll be much more comfortable at Mrs E's house than here," he said, running a critical eye over the façade. Just as well he couldn't see Joe's truck from here. His sleek silver car didn't even look like it came from the same planet. "Do you want me to come in with you?"

"I'm fine. I won't be long." I got out of the low-slung car with relief. Just sharing the same air as someone like that left a bad taste in my mouth.

I flicked on the light as I came in. To my surprise, Syl was already awake, sitting up glaring at me.

What sort of time is this to be coming home, young lady?

"Very funny. You won't believe the night I've had." I started stuffing clothes into my backpack. "Shit's getting way too real out there."

She eyed my preparations suspiciously. *Are we going somewhere?*

"Turns out Adrian is with the bad guys, and they've got Jake."

She hissed. *I told you not to trust those One Worlder bastards. So much for let's play happy Aristaeans together.*

"I'm *not* an Aristaean," I snapped, "and those are *not* my people. They're worse than One Worlders—they're shadow shapers. They can't help me find my mother, or my past—but they might be able to destroy my future." My hands trembled as I shoved the last of my few belongings into the pack. I would *not* let the shadow shapers have that irritating, untrusting, gorgeous fireshaper. "Please, Syl. It's *Jake*. I need your help."

I shouldered the backpack and grabbed Joe's keys off the bedside table.

What are you planning?

"We're going hunting."

We are? What for?

"A key."

13

Mrs Emery's house contained a dozen bedrooms, each with their own bathroom, as the man who showed me to my room explained. Apparently, I had been given the very best one available. By that time, it was so late it was early, and I was so tired I could have slept on the floor, but I made the appropriate noises of appreciation as I followed him upstairs, carrying Syl in my arms. He kept a wary distance from "the animal", and Syl treated him to the death stare the whole way. He departed in a hurry as soon as we'd arrived at my room, but maybe he was just keen to get to his own bed. I fell on top of mine, fully dressed, and promptly lost consciousness.

When I woke, the room was bright with daylight and the baleful red numbers on the clock radio by the bed said 8:45. I would have liked to sleep longer, but time was ticking away. Jake needed me. I bet he hadn't slept on a soft bed.

I rubbed sleep out of my gritty eyes and sent my awareness out through the house, but I had no more luck than I'd had last night at finding other eyes to turn to my purposes.

"One spider in the whole house," I complained to Syl. "These people are such neat freaks." I got up and stretched, taking some deep breaths to try to wake myself up. Coffee. I needed coffee. "Never mind, there's more than one way to kill a cat."

Hey! Watch your language.

"Come on, let's go find some coffee."

You should give that shit up, she said, but she jumped down from the bed and followed me out into the hallway. *You're addicted to it.*

You're just jealous because you haven't had any in months. I switched to my inner voice as we moved through the house. These people already thought I was weird for having a cat—if they found me talking to it, too, they'd think I'd completely lost it. No point making them suspicious until I had to.

Says the girl mooning over the hot fireshaper.

I am not mooning. I stalked down the stairs, Syl trailing behind like a bad smell, only to find Adrian waiting at the bottom.

"Good morning," he said. "I hope you slept well."

"Very well, thank you." No thanks to him. It was a

wonder I hadn't had nightmares after that scene in the cellar.

"Come and have some breakfast."

He led me into a downstairs room that overlooked a pretty little grove of trees. A path wound through the trees down to the lake at the back of the house. Two men seated at the table looked up as we entered, eyeing me speculatively as they said good morning. A buffet breakfast was laid out on the sideboard, where I poured myself a cup of coffee and drank it so fast I scalded the back of my throat. Adrian sat down as I helped myself to croissants from a tray of baked goods.

Is he going to watch you eat? Syl asked, slinking under the table as I sat too.

Looks that way. I just hope he's not going to get in the way. Mrs Emery had told him not to let me out of his sight, and he seemed to be taking the command seriously. I had a feeling she wasn't only concerned for my welfare, despite her apparent gratitude. She wouldn't have got where she was by being trusting, and part of Adrian's brief was no doubt to keep an eye on me to make sure I didn't get up to anything untoward.

After the meal, he took me on an exhaustive tour of the mansion, and then asked me what I'd like to do for the rest of the day.

"Anything you like," he said. "I'm completely at your disposal."

Damn it, he was going to be a pain in the arse. "Actually, I think I might go back to bed. I'm still awfully tired."

"Of course," he said, accompanying me up the stairs. For a moment, I thought he meant to stand guard outside my room, but he stopped at the door opposite mine. "I might have a bit of a rest myself. Call me if there's anything you need." He waited there, smiling, until I'd gone into my own room and shut the door.

Now what? asked Syl.

"Now we wait," I said grimly, my eyes on the clock at the bedside. Time was ticking away, and I'd made no progress yet. Damn Adrian, and damn Mrs Emery. Untrusting bitch.

When I figured enough time had passed, I eased the door open. No sign of Adrian. As quietly as I could, I crept from the room and back down the stairs, Syl at my heels.

Outside, I zipped my jacket right up to the top; the morning air had a sharp bite to it though the sun was well on towards midday.

What are we doing out here? Syl asked.

Looking for mice.

Awesome. I love mice.

Not to eat, Syl. I need to get some creatures into that house to use as eyes and ears.

She sat down in the pathway and stared up at me mutinously. *You could use me. Then I could eat the mice.*

I plan on using you. But you're not small enough to get into every nook and cranny. And there were those massive cellars, stretching away under the house into the dark. *Believe me, there's more to this place than meets the eye. There's a lot to search, and we don't have much time. And besides, I'm sure we can find you something better for breakfast than mice.*

There's nothing better for breakfast than mice, she objected. *Nothing tastes better than a meal you've caught yourself.*

I strode off down the gravel path, unsettled. She never used to say things like that before she started spending every moment as a cat. *What about avocado on toast? Bacon and eggs? Or granola with fresh strawberries? Oh, right, I forgot, you're just a cat. You don't eat any of that human shit.*

I don't have to answer to you for the form I choose, she snapped. *Anyone would think you didn't like shifters, the way you carry on.*

She stalked off ahead, outrage in every line of her body, but I had no time for this argument now. I could feel that clock ticking away the moments until nightfall, when the house would fill with people again. I had to find the key and be far away from here with Jake before then. Before the murderous Mrs Emery turned up with her captive god. Clearly, even a fireshaper was no match for her and her nasty silver collars. What the hell could I do with only a grumpy cat for help?

Twenty minutes later, I returned to the house with three brown field mice snuggled together in my jacket pocket. I'd found some beetles, too, scuttling among the fallen leaves by the lakeside, and these I called to me as I entered the house. They zipped past me through the open door, the sun glinting on their glossy black carapaces as they flew. The men who'd been eating breakfast had gone. I snagged another croissant as I passed, and went out into the hallway, scattering little flakes of pastry and buttery goodness in my wake. I sent the beetles scuttling under the fake bookcase door and down into the dark, while Syl and I ascended the stairs to the guest bedrooms.

Start with Mrs Emery's room, I told her. *That's the most likely place for the safe.*

I waited until she'd disappeared around the corner before releasing the mice, then headed for my own room.

Adrian's door opened as I reached it, and he frowned at the sight of me in the corridor. "I thought you were going to sleep?"

"Oh, I am. Just felt a little hungry still." I held up the last of my croissant as proof. He nodded and went back into his room—but this time he didn't shut his door.

Well, that was going to make sneaking out trickier. He was certainly taking guard duty seriously. Still, that was a problem for later.

I locked my own door and lay down again on the bed,

but this time sleep was off the menu. Instead, I focused on the little sparks of animal awareness I'd seeded through the house, guiding the mice to show me the world through their eyes. Syl I left to herself; she would alert me if she found something.

It was disorienting to switch frequently between several sets of eyes, but I didn't have time for a leisurely exploration. One of the mice found a mouse-sized hole and had to be prodded into action—he was too close to Syl, and the smell of cat was making him nervous. I sent him scurrying in the other direction, squeezing under the closed door of one of the guest suites.

The rooms the mice showed me were all as luxurious as the one I had. Carefully, we examined each one for any likely hiding places, paying particular attention to any paintings. A lot of people were like the Ruby Adept, and hid their safes behind paintings. But I also had the mice sneaking into wardrobes and under beds, clambering over shelves and sniffing for anything that smelled as though it didn't belong.

Mrs Emery's door is shut, Syl said into my mind.

So open it, I said, distracted by some rather perilous climbing by one of my little friends.

No opposable thumbs, remember? came the tart reply.

Is there anyone around?

No.

Then shift.

Can't you come and do it?

I've got Adrian watching my every move. You're just going to have to grow a set, Syl.

Gods above, Lexi, you could try a little compassion. What if somebody sees me?

No one's going to see you. You just said no one was around! And I'm sorry, but I'm all out of compassion for your hang-ups. Jake's life is at stake here. Just do it, Syl.

Fine, she huffed. And a moment later: *I'm in.*

Well, thank God. Obviously she hadn't stayed human, since our mind link only worked when she was in cat form, but I'd been afraid she really wouldn't do it.

Eager to see what she saw, I abandoned the mice for the moment and flew down our link. Mrs Emery's bedroom was twice as large as mine. Gold wallpaper glittered in the sunlight streaming in the big bay window. A brass four-poster bed stood in the centre of the white-carpeted floor, piled high with cushions in gold and white tonings. Behind it, a low parapet separated the bedroom from an open bathroom boasting a large claw-footed bath. Anyone sitting in the bath would have a lovely view out the bay window and over the lake. Just as well Mrs Emery hadn't been bathing when I'd been wandering around down there earlier collecting mice.

Check behind the paintings, I said.

There were two. One was a landscape with the sun setting behind distant hills, done in pinks and golds. The other was a portrait of a young woman in a white ball gown and tiara, staring out into the distance as if contemplating the mysteries of the universe. Or maybe she was constipated. It was kind of a distracted look. I had no idea who she was, though it clearly wasn't Mrs Emery. Even when she was younger, Mrs Emery wouldn't have looked that beautiful.

I know what I'm doing, Syl grumbled, still pissed at me for making her shift.

Syl got up nice and close, even standing up on her hind legs to peer behind the paintings, but there was nothing there but wallpaper. Undeterred, we checked the whole room, including around the vanity in the bathroom and inside the walk-in wardrobe. Syl leapt up onto the top shelf in the wardrobe. That was also a favourite hiding spot with many people, with boxes of valuables shoved to the back, out of sight from the floor below. No luck.

Maybe she has an office downstairs, Syl suggested.

I left her there and flitted after the mice. My stomach was rumbling despite the croissant, telling me it was nearly lunchtime, but we'd made a thorough search of the top floor. The mice, unsupervised, had gravitated toward the food smells coming from the kitchen. I set them to work again, though really the office was the only likely place on that level. The kitchen was too busy and full of staff, while the conference room and the big function and reception rooms were too public.

Sadly, the office yielded no treasures. It didn't look as though Mrs Emery spent much time there—it was too pristine. A group of men in business suits had gathered in the dining room where breakfast had been laid out, and tension gnawed at my stomach. People were starting to arrive already for the evening's big event, and I was no closer to freeing Jake.

I dove down into the dark below the house and located my beetles. Time to start cutting corners. I could tell from the way sound echoed in the beetles' hearing that the search area was vast. The cellars seemed to extend much further than the footprint of the house above. If the safe was down here, where was the most likely place for it?

Syl butted into my thoughts. *Hey, look who's here.*

I dove back into her head. She was sitting demurely in the hallway outside Mrs Emery's doorway, and two people were approaching: Bruno and Irene. Irene gave a little squeak of horror when she saw Syl.

"What is that horrible creature doing there?"

"I heard that girl of Adrian's brought her." He stamped his foot. "Scat! Get out of here!"

Ignorant piece of shit, Syl said. She sat down and began to lick her front paw as if she were completely alone.

"I don't like her," Irene said, presumably meaning me and not the cat. I couldn't say I was too broken-hearted to hear it. I didn't like Irene either. "Why should she waltz in at the last moment and get a piece of the pie? She hasn't been working her arse off like the rest of us. And now we're expected to share the rewards with her?"

"It's not as though there won't be enough to go around," Bruno said mildly. He kept a wary eye on the cat as they walked past, as if he expected Syl to make a sudden leap for his jugular. "Apollo *is* one of the twelve Olympians, after all."

"Yes, but every extra person dilutes the power," Irene objected. "I don't see why *I* should have less, just to accommodate her. I've earned this. And don't you think it's odd we haven't heard of her before?"

"I've asked Gerald to send me a list of all the Aristaeans. We'll soon know if she really is one. We only have Adrian's word for it at the moment—and you know he'd do anything to get on Mrs Emery's good side."

"Little brown nose," Irene said, and then she squealed again and nearly climbed into Bruno's arms as one of my mice scurried across the corridor in front of her.

She turned and glared at Syl, who gave her an insolent stare in return.

"Honestly, what is the point of a cat that doesn't even chase mice? Nasty beast."

They headed for the stairs, Irene sticking close to Bruno's protection.

She's a real charmer, Syl said, staring after them. *Should I trip her down the stairs?*

It's tempting. I didn't like the fact that they were suspicious of me, but it was hardly surprising. Suspicion seemed to run in these people's veins. *I wonder how long it will take for this list of Aristaeans to come through?*

Syl's mental tone was gloomy. *Probably not bloody long enough.*

❦

An annoying electronic beeping brought me back to my own senses. I opened my eyes to find the clock radio having some kind of breakdown. As well as the noise, it was flashing numbers at me—random numbers that bore no relation to the time of day, which my stomach was insisting was after lunch. 25:86. 39:17. Twenty-five o'clock, right. What next? Would all the clocks strike thirteen and propel us into another world? I hit the off button, but the damn noise wouldn't stop, so I pulled the power cord. The next occupant of the room could deal with it.

Closing my eyes again, I sent the beetles scurrying through the cellars, following the path we'd taken the night before. If I was lucky, something would jump out at me and save me a lot of time. I was horribly conscious of the time, even if the clock radio had decided to throw in the towel.

But there were no helpful flashing signs saying SAFE HIDDEN HERE, so we edged past the big stone altar, still crusted with dried blood, and continued down the corridor that they'd dragged the god from last night. It wasn't very long, but it was dim, lit by a single globe that struggled to illuminate the whole length. Two heavy wooden doors stood on each side of the corridor, with another at the end. Fortunately, they all had a big enough gap at the bottom to allow a beetle to squeeze underneath and into the room beyond.

The rooms behind the first two doors seemed to be used as storage, though it was too dark to see much, even for the beetles, other than the looming shapes of boxes and barrels. The dust on the floor was undisturbed, though, so it seemed safe not to explore any further.

The first room on the right smelled of blood and sweat and a toilet that hadn't been cleaned in a long time. The beetle stopped as I took in the sight of the room's occupant, slumped in a sullen heap on a dirty mattress on the floor.

Jake had his back to the brick wall, knees drawn up and arms resting loosely on them. The silver collar gleamed dully in the light of a single globe overhead. At least they hadn't left him in the dark. As I watched, he reached up and tugged at the collar, running his fingers underneath it.

From the angry red marks on his neck, he'd been doing this a while, until now he did it from habit rather than from any real expectation of being able to break free of its restraint. It must be a new experience for someone like him to be so powerless.

Then I remembered the scars on his back, and Adrian describing his last spell in captivity. No, not a new experience. No wonder he looked so bleak. He knew exactly what to expect from these people, and mercy wasn't on the menu.

My heart clenched with fear for him, and I drew the beetle away. I wanted to soothe that awful look from his face, but there was no time. The only way I could help was to find that key.

One of my beetles had slipped my control and gone meandering up the wall at the beginning of the corridor. When it found a key hanging on a hook there, I nearly lost control of it again in a burst of shock and hope. But of course it wasn't the key to Jake's collar—no one would leave such an important thing lying around so openly. Besides, once I'd recovered myself, I could see it was too big for that. It was an ordinary door key, and, with any luck, it opened the door to Jake's cell.

It was about time I had some good luck. The safe still remained elusive, and time was not on our side. We checked the other rooms beyond Jake's, with no success.

Syl interrupted me to demand admittance to my bedroom, so I got up and unlocked the door for her, then went straight back to work.

We searched the room with all the barrels, where Jake and I had hidden to watch the beginning of the ceremony the night before. I sent those beetles crawling under every barrel and into every little nook and cranny, searching for hidden panels in the floor or walls. No luck.

"What's the time?" I asked Syl, yawning as I came back to myself.

She looked pointedly at the blank face of the unplugged clock radio, then out the window. *Looks like mid-afternoon. You'd better hurry it up.*

"Those cellars are so big. What if it's not even down there? Maybe she keeps it at another location. We could search all day and still find nothing." The urge to move, to take *some* kind of action, was nagging at me, making me feel all jumpy and unsettled. "I found the key to his cell. Maybe we should just break him out of there and worry about getting the collar off later."

She eyed me dubiously, her head tipped to one side. *If those things are designed to hold a god powerless, I have the feeling you won't just be able to get one off with a hacksaw.*

I got off the bed and began to pace. "Hades might be able to help." We should just do it. Every minute Jake spent locked in that cell was another minute wasted.

And he might not, either. Her mental tone was tart. *I know your impulse control is no better than the average two-year-old's, but do try to think this through. This house is full of shadow shapers. You don't even know what powers they have, but they're all going to turn on you the minute you unlock that cell door. There are barely any animals around for you to work with. How exactly do you think we're going to escape this place without Fire Boy being able to do his thing? I mean, he's pretty and all, but he's not much use without his powers.*

I stopped pacing and returned her glare with interest, but it's hard to out-glare a cat, particularly when I had to admit she was right. "There's still so much to search down there. The damn cellars go on forever."

Have you looked in the first room at the bottom of the stairs? Seems to me no one is going to want to traipse for miles in the dark every time they want to access their safe.

I'd given that room a cursory inspection, but perhaps in my haste to get to the corridor where Jake was being held, I hadn't been as thorough as I might have.

"I'll have another look."

Marshalling the beetle troops, I sent them exploring behind every barrel, and examined every flagstone in the floor of the room in question.

In the end, the damn thing was in the shadows beneath the staircase.

I leapt up. "Found it!"

Syl caught my excitement and bounced to her feet. *Where?*

"Under the stairs. There's a wooden panel set into the brick wall. It's got to be behind that."

See? Repeat after me: Syl is always right.

I rolled my eyes but wasted no more time; there was little enough left. I cracked the door open, but Adrian was still in his room across the hall, door wide open. He was watching TV, but that wouldn't last if he saw me come out. I shut the door again with a muttered expletive.

Adrian still on guard?

"Yes. Bastard."

I grabbed my backpack and heaved the window open instead. My room was at the side of the house, above a covered outdoor area. It was the work of a moment to climb out onto that roof, then swing down to the ground.

Syl trotting at my heels, I went round to the back of the house and let myself back inside. Two men loitered in the book-lined corridor, not far from the secret door. They fell silent as I strode past and into the huge room with the two-storey fireplace, trying to look as though I had somewhere important to be. They eyed my cat and my backpack with equal interest.

Now what? Syl asked.

Now we wait. As soon as the coast is clear, we're through that bookcase faster than you can say cats are bossy shitheads.

She regarded me through narrowed green eyes, but chose to ignore my taunt. *Would you like me to hiss at them and hurry proceedings along?*

Let's not alarm them any more than we have to. I shifted impatiently from one foot to the other while Syl watched the corridor.

Now, she said, at last.

Okay, so we probably had time to say *cats are bossy shitheads* twice by the time I cracked open the bookcase door and we both slipped through, but it was still fast. I closed the door behind us and leaned on it for a moment, listening, but no shouts of surprise or alarm sounded in the corridor we'd just left. After the well-lit hallway, it was pitch black this side of the door, so I waited until my eyes adjusted before following Syl down the stairs, making full use of my borrowed night vision.

I didn't dare turn on the light at the bottom, but I had a flashlight in my backpack, and I was soon playing its beam across the wooden panel under the staircase. There was a small recess on either side of it, and when I stuck my fingers in them the panel lifted away easily, revealing the safe behind it.

We don't know the code, Syl said, regarding the keypad doubtfully.

I shone the light into the recesses of my pack, digging down deep. "Not a problem. I still have that little gizmo that Jake made for me."

The gizmo was about the size of a hand grenade, completely flat on one side, with a button on the more rounded face. He'd given it to me to blow the Ruby Adept's safe, when I was trying to steal Apollo's damned ring—only the ring had turned out to be on the Ruby Adept's finger, and the little device had gone unused.

But not unappreciated. I'd kept it with my other tools, since you never knew when something like that might come in handy.

"It's magnetic, see?" I held it against the safe's smooth surface and felt it lock into place. "Now all I have to do is press this button and step back."

Syl leapt away as I pressed the button, and I wasn't far behind. Jake had said it was perfectly safe to remain in the same room, as the blast was directed inward, but I was taking no chances.

There was a moment's silence.

And then it goes kaboom? Syl asked.

"That's the idea." I waited, counting off the seconds in my head. *A few seconds*, he'd said. The little device clung to the outside of the safe, completely still. How many was *a few*? Twenty? Thirty? I got to a minute, then two. Still nothing.

It seems to be lacking in the kaboom department, Syl said, when a full five minutes had passed. *Maybe it's broken. Or maybe it doesn't work because it's connected to his shaping ability and that collar is stopping him from shaping.*

185

"Maybe." I had a sick feeling in my gut, a sense of doom rushing down on us. I didn't care *why* it didn't work, only that it didn't. I'd found the safe, the key was right there in front of me—but I couldn't get to it.

Our lives depended on me opening that safe. Plan A had now failed, and I had no Plan B.

14

"Looks like we'll have to break him out and take our chances with the shadow shapers—without his powers to protect us," I said.

That sounded like a really bad option, but I couldn't see any other way. A desperate, panicky feeling was eating at me, making it hard to think. I kept seeing Zephyrus lying on that altar again, his blood splashing on the hard earth floor, only this time he wore Jake's face. I couldn't fail him—I *couldn't*.

If we went out the door that opened to the garden, we might be able to get away without being noticed. This area was pretty rural; perhaps we could find a barn to lay low in, or a truck to steal—country people sometimes left the keys to their vehicles tucked into the sun visor, or even hanging in the ignition.

Can't you crack it? she asked, gazing hopefully at the keypad. *You've done that before.*

"Usually I just find the combination written somewhere obvious, like in the front of a desk diary." People were so predictable—and lazy. But I'd already seen the unused state of Mrs Emery's office. There weren't likely to be any handy clues waiting for me there. And I didn't know her well enough to try to guess, based on her birthdate or the ages of her children, or any of the other tricks people used to help them remember. She probably didn't even *have* children. She would have been too busy making fortunes and crushing the souls of her opposition underfoot to have time for childbearing. "And this make has an eight-digit combination. That's too many possibilities for trial and error."

Eight digits: four groups of two. The first two had to be twenty or greater. Other than that, it was open slather. No way could I fluke that. But Syl just stared at me with her big green eyes, looking all lost and appealing.

Half-heartedly I punched in a string of numbers: 67-99-42-33. Of course, the door didn't open when I tried it.

Take off the gizmo, she suggested.

As if that would make any difference. But I took it off and punched in another random sequence, starting with 20, my own age: 20-58-17-08.

Now would be a really good time for Hades to show up with a bright idea. I'd even welcome Cerberus at this point. We could do with the firepower. Or Athena. The goddess of wisdom might have a few pointers for me on the fine art of safe-cracking. What I needed was my own personal god to supply me with clues whenever I prayed to them.

Like whoever had given me the message on the TV screens in that shop window. Not that "beware ring" had been that useful as a message. A nice little string of numbers would have been much better.

And then I froze.

What's up? Syl asked, but I ignored her.

A nice little string of numbers. With the first one greater than twenty. Like twenty-five o'clock.

I bolted for the stairs. Maybe I *did* have someone sending me helpful messages. I just hadn't recognised it for what it was.

A handy mouse showed me that the coast was clear before we opened the bookcase door. Voices came from the dining room, and another group were laughing in the big reception room with the two-storey fireplace. No one saw us as we ducked outside and scaled the pillar to the low roof and back through my window.

What are you doing? Syl asked, grumpy and confused.

"Praying for a miracle," I said, as I plugged the clock radio back in. The first number had been twenty-five, but I couldn't remember the rest of the sequence. *Please, please.*

A red 12:00 appeared, flashing, and my heart sank. Too

189

late, then. I sank down on the bed, out of breath and out of hope.

Then the numbers changed. 25:86 flashed up, followed by 39:17.

"That's it," I said, watching as the sequence cycled through again. "That's the code for the safe."

Okay, this shit is just getting weird now. Syl backed away, stiff-legged. *Why is your alarm clock talking to you?*

I headed for the window, renewed energy flooding my body. "I don't think it is. Someone is using it to send me a message."

How is that even possible? It's a clock, not a flipping phone. Her ears lay flat against her head. *Are you telling me someone is watching us right now? Listening to our conversations? How the hell can they do that?*

Don't ask me. I switched to mental speech as we climbed out the window again. To be honest, the thought that someone, however benign, seemed to be spying on us somehow made me more than a little nervous—but hey, if they were going to help us, I'd take anything I could get. *Maybe Jake knows.*

The thought of freeing Jake and getting out of this place made my heart lift as we slipped once more through the bookcase door and down the dark stairs. Heart in my mouth, I punched in the sequence of numbers our mysterious benefactor had supplied: 25-86-39-17. The beep that greeted this sequence was the sweetest sound I'd ever heard. I pulled open the door and there it was: the key I'd seen Mrs Emery use so briefly the night before. It was small and plain but in my eyes it was beautiful.

I hurried through the dark cellar with it clutched in my fist. The other key, the one I hoped would open Jake's door, still hung on its hook at the corner of the prisoners' corridor. "You stay here," I whispered to Syl. "Let me know if anyone comes."

She nodded, and wandered back into the darkness underneath the altar while I slipped around the corner, a key in each hand.

The big key did indeed open Jake's door. Score one for the good guys. He looked up as the door opened, a scowl on his face, which only deepened when he saw it was me.

"What do *you* want?" he growled. "Come to gloat?"

"Nice," I said. "I wasn't expecting backflips, but a little more excitement is usually expected when someone breaks in to rescue you."

"You have a key," he pointed out. "No doubt supplied by your Shadower friends. That's not breaking in."

His scowl was so daunting I hesitated. He might not have his powers any more, but he was still a big guy. Bigger when he stood up, as he did now. He glanced past me at the open door, as if he were calculating his chances of knocking me down and making a break for freedom.

"This one was hanging on a nail outside." I opened my hand to show him the other one. "But *this* one, I had to steal."

He stared at it, his expression flat and hard. "Is this some kind of trick?"

I blew out a frustrated breath. "Oh, come on, Jake. You didn't really believe I'd betrayed you, did you? You're going to have to decide, once and for all, whether you trust me or not. This flip-flopping back and forth is giving me the shits." After what we'd been through together, that look on his face really hurt. I'd risked death for him, and he'd done the same for me. A little faith might have been nice. "Would it have been better if I'd let them lock me up in here with you? Then we'd both be screwed, and we wouldn't be having this conversation, because I wouldn't have just busted my gut to find a way to get that thing off you, you ungrateful sod."

His face softened, though his eyes were still wary. "I didn't *want* to believe it, but I never know where I am with you. You stole the damn ring—what was I supposed to think?"

"I like to think of it more as *borrowing*," I said, stepping closer and gesturing for him to turn around so I could reach the lock. "I gave it back to you, didn't I?"

"You are the most infuriating person I've ever met," he growled over his shoulder. "You drive me crazy."

The lock clicked and the collar snapped open. "Well, that's not a very long journey, is it? All you shapers are nuts."

He pulled the collar off and flexed his fingers. Little tongues of fire sprang to life on each fingertip. A satisfied grin split his face. "*That's* more like it."

"Great." Fire Boy was back. "Let's get out of here."

I started for the door but he caught at my hand. "Wait."

Wait? "Much as I like holding hands with you, we're kind of running out of time here."

His mouth quirked, and his thumb caressed the back of my hand, but he refused to be diverted. "The guy who brought me water said they were sacrificing Apollo tonight. We can't leave without him."

"Well, he's not here yet, and I can hardly come back and rescue you when he is. The place will be crawling with shadow shapers. We need to leave *now*." There were already more shadow shapers upstairs than I liked. Once Mrs Emery arrived with the god, there'd be more, and I doubted they'd leave Apollo conveniently alone down here. The party would get started as soon as he arrived. "I think we've already demonstrated that the two of us alone are outmatched here."

"They caught me by surprise. That won't happen again." He stared at the collar in his hand, turning it around to examine the lock. "I could put this back on so they don't suspect anything and keep the key in my pocket."

And break out and cause havoc when they least expected it. That could work. Except—

"What if they search you before the ceremony?"

"Why would they? They've already done that."

"Well, what if they take your clothes off?"

"They didn't take Zephyrus's clothes off."

"That doesn't mean they'll do it the same way tonight. Besides, if they handcuff you before they let you out of this cell, you're screwed. It's too risky, Jake. Can't you—I don't know—disable the collar in some way?"

"You think I haven't tried that? Whoever created this is a lot more powerful than me. It's completely impervious to my shaping."

"Then we have to go."

"I'm not going anywhere without Apollo." A desperate fear lurked in his eyes. "He's my *god*, Lexi. I can't leave him to be slaughtered like a dog. These people aren't fit to touch his hand—they have no right to steal his powers."

"We'll come back for him."

"If I escape now, they'll double their security. We'll have no chance of getting Apollo out. I have to stay."

Damn the man. And he thought *I* was infuriating. What did I do now?

What's the hold-up? Syl asked. *We can't hang around here forever, you know.*

I know! A blast of frustration surged down our link.

Bloody Jake is being all noble and refusing to leave without Apollo. He's got some crackpot scheme of putting the collar back on and just hoping he gets a chance to unlock it before they both get slaughtered.

Sounds risky. Too bad he can't copy it, like he did with the ring.

My knees went weak with relief. *Syl, I could kiss you!*

Thanks, but you can save that kind of stuff for Hotpants there.

I gazed at Jake, a stupid grin spreading over my face.

"What?" he asked suspiciously. "That look usually means trouble."

"Not trouble—a much better plan. What if you made a fake collar? Then there'd be no danger of not getting an opportunity to use the key, or having the key taken from you."

"That would be a great idea, if I only had access to some metal."

"These cellars are full of barrels." They were made of wood, but they all had big rings of iron holding the wood into shape. "Couldn't you take the metal from those?"

"They wouldn't be the right colour. I don't even know what this metal is—it looks like pewter, but it's not. I think someone would notice if my collar suddenly changed colour."

Damn. It had been such a good idea. "Wait—" Another possibility occurred to me. "I'll be right back."

I left him there and hurried back through the darkness.

Where's lover boy? Syl asked, falling into step beside me. *Is he coming or not?*

This is just a side trip, I assured her, unlocking the door that led out into the gardens and easing it open. *Won't be long.*

I slipped out into the afternoon sunshine. The shadows lay long across the lawn at the side of the house, and here under the trees the air was cool. Soon it would be dark, and Mrs Emery's gory ceremony would begin. Was she here already? There were more cars parked beside the driveway than before, though still not as many as last night. Hopefully that meant we still had time, and no one was hammering on my bedroom door wondering why I didn't answer.

I was looking for one car in particular, and felt a thrill of glee when I saw its sleek silver lines: Adrian's car. It was almost exactly the colour of the collar, and I wandered over to where it was parked, trying to look as if I was just out for a stroll.

No one was watching—at least that I could tell. Perhaps my mysterious benefactor had some way of seeing what I was up to, but I doubted he or she would object to a spot of vandalism. I took hold of the side mirror of Adrian's very sleek, very expensive car and twisted and pulled and shoved until it came off in my hands, trailing electrical wiring. Such a good colour.

I hurried back to the cellar, feeling horribly exposed until I got inside and the darkness closed around me again.

"Will this do?" I asked, still breathing heavily from my exertions.

Jake took it and smiled. "Someone isn't going to be happy when they see what you've done to their car."

I grinned too, picturing Adrian's face. Served the bastard right. "If we manage to pull this off, he'll have a lot more to be unhappy about than the state of his car."

15

It was a select group gathered around the bloodstained altar in the cellar that night. Adrian, Bruno, Irene, and I formed a loose circle with Crawshaw, the newspaper mogul, and the property developer guy, whose name I'd forgotten, but who'd sat next to Mrs Emery at the gala dinner the night before. There was no sign of Matt, who presumably wasn't considered important enough to be given a piece of the sun god's power, since he hadn't even gotten to share in Zephyrus's. Newton, the CEO of EmeryCorp, was there, too, and it was due to his eagerness that we were all standing around in the dank cellar rather than waiting upstairs in comfort for Mrs Emery to arrive with the god. She'd rung him to say she was only ten minutes away, and he'd hustled us down to the cellar faster than you could say "sacrifice time".

Most of the guests had brought their drinks with them,

and there was a festive feel in the air. Irene flirted with Newton, tossing her blonde hair seductively over her shoulder, while Bruno engaged Crawshaw in conversation about stocks and shares, which sounded duller than ditch water to me, but they appeared to be enjoying it.

By my side, Adrian was practically quivering with excitement. "I can't believe this moment has finally come! We've waited so long."

"Mmm," I said, noncommittally. It was all I could do to keep the smile plastered on my face. My insides were quivering, too, but with nerves, not excitement. Jake was waiting in his cell, wearing the fake collar. He hadn't been able to make a perfect replica, since the colouring was only on the surface and not part of the actual metal. Working the metal into its new shape without damaging the paintwork had taken a lot out of him; I could see him flagging as he worked on it. As a result, the finished collar had some dodgy patches on the back where the darker underlying colour showed through. Hopefully no one would be looking that closely at his collar, though, once the god arrived.

The plan was simple: once Apollo arrived and they brought Jake from his cell, Jake would attack with fire, aiming to take Mrs Emery out of play, while I used the key I had shoved in my bra to free Apollo from his collar. Once Apollo had access to his powers again, it would be game over for Mrs Emery and her crowd of corporate killers. Syl was hiding behind the wine barrels in the next room with the spare collar, in case we needed it for any particularly recalcitrant shadow shapers, though, privately, I doubted she would even have the guts to turn human long enough to carry it in here. If they didn't bring Jake out in time, he would break out of his cell instead, which would be easy for him to do now he could shape again—all it would take was a little metalshaping of the lock. It was a nice, simple plan.

I heartily approved of simple plans, but the simplicity of this one was deceptive. There were too many unknowns on the other side. Everyone else in this cellar had powers, but I didn't know what they were. They'd all stolen the god of the west wind's powers the night before, so airshaping should be on the menu, but who knew what else they could do? If any of them had been there when Hephaistos was killed, for instance, they'd be able to metalshape, too, possibly better than Jake could now the god was dead. And depending on which other gods they'd murdered, they could have all sorts of strange and wonderful abilities.

Plus, if any of them were armed ... we'd already proved that fireshapers were as susceptible to bullets as regular humans. If their shaping abilities weren't enough to stop Jake, a single bullet would do the job just as well.

I glanced into the shadows on the other side of the archway. I wasn't the only one looking that way, though the others were anticipating the arrival of Mrs Emery and Apollo. I was making sure that Syl was well hidden with the spare collar. I was looking forward to seeing that collar shining around Mrs Emery's neck, and I hoped it choked her.

Everything okay back there? I asked Syl.

Fine. Although this dust is making me want to sneeze. I hope they get here soon. This place stinks.

I hoped so, too, though not because of the pervasive smell of sour wine. I clasped my hands together to keep them from trembling.

Despite the bright chatter and the smiles, there was a tension in the air. Everyone knew what was coming next. For some, this was clearly the culmination of a long-held dream. Adrian's eyes were bright, almost fevered. Sick bastard. Bruno was harder to read, but Irene was positively triumphant. Her gaze continually darted to the cushion that rested on the altar, bearing the familiar sunburst ring.

How I longed to snatch that ring and make a run for it. But Jake was adamant that we had to save the god who owned it, so I waited, though my legs twitched with the effort of standing still here among these smiling killers.

I nearly jumped out of my skin when Bruno's phone suddenly shrilled from his pocket.

Adrian laid a reassuring hand on my arm. "Nervous?"

"A little."

Bruno checked the caller ID, then looked straight at me before leaving the room to take the call. Uh-oh. What was that about?

"Don't be. In a few minutes, the long wait will be over, and all our efforts will bear fruit."

He could take his fruit and jam it sideways. I removed my arm from his grasp, watching the archway for Bruno's reappearance.

Can you hear what Bruno's saying? I asked Syl. *He gave me a funny look when his phone rang.*

He's gone outside and shut the door. Do you think it's something about Aristaeans?

That's what I'm afraid of. He'd said earlier that he was going to make enquiries. Just a few more minutes—that was all I needed. If he held off his accusations until Apollo arrived, it wouldn't matter any more what he'd discovered.

Here he comes, Syl said. *That was quick.*

Quick, and probably not good news for me, judging by the triumphant stare he gave me as he walked back in. I tensed, waiting for the denunciation, the big reveal that I was not who I said I was. But he merely murmured something to Irene and slipped his phone back into his pocket. So, we were going to wait for Mrs Emery to arrive to duke this out? Suited me just fine.

Right on cue, there was a commotion at the outer door, followed by footfalls on the packed earth floor—three or four people approaching. The group in the cellar fell silent, watching the archway with anticipation.

She's here, Syl said, unnecessarily, because in a moment I could see for myself. Mrs Emery appeared out of the darkness, accompanied by two men supporting a third in between them. I couldn't see his face because his head drooped, lank hair falling forward to cover his features, but the collar around his neck told me who he was, if I'd needed any further clues. Apollo, Lord of the Sun and one of the twelve great gods of Olympus, was looking more than a little worse for wear. Smelled it, too— judging by his rank aroma, he hadn't bathed in quite some time. His T-shirt had probably started life as white, but it was now an indeterminate grey, and his jeans were filthy. His bare feet were crusted in dirt and he was so skinny that a decent gust of wind could have blown him away.

Mrs Emery's sharp gaze swept around the circle. She wore a business suit and the same silver cuff peeked out of its sleeve that I'd noticed the night before. When she nodded at Newton, he leapt forward to help the two bodyguards manhandle Apollo onto the altar. He was virtually a dead weight, as if his scrawny body had no energy left. Irene whipped the cushion bearing his avatar out of the way as the god slumped down on the cold stone. I don't think he even saw the ring. Now that he was stretched out on his back, I could see his eyes were closed, as if he'd resigned himself to this fate long ago and just didn't want to watch it coming for him. Poor bastard. He'd been a captive a long time. A surge of sympathy for him rose in my heart. His dirty blonde hair would have been nearly the same shade as my brother's if it had been clean, and my hatred for these brutal shadow shapers ratcheted up another notch.

"I'm sorry to keep you waiting, but I'm sure you'll all agree it was worth the wait," Mrs Emery said. Smiles and nods greeted this pronouncement. She frowned as she looked around the circle of faces. "Are we all here?"

The bodyguards had cuffed Apollo to the altar. He lay on his back, eyes closed, as if he were already dead.

"Everyone on the list," Newton said, with a small matching frown. Probably worried that he might have displeased his boss. She didn't seem like the type who dealt well with being disappointed. "Why?"

"If we're all here, who's out there?"

Before I knew what she was about, she'd marched back into the room beyond the arch and dived behind a pile of barrels. She moved fast, considering the height of the heels she wore. My heart constricted as a yowl rent the air, followed by a hiss. Triumphant, she emerged from behind the barrels with Syl dangling from one hand, caught by the scruff of her neck. Mrs Emery's arm dripped blood from a series of scratches, and her smart business suit was smeared with dust, but that was small consolation. Syl's green eyes met mine, desperation in them.

"Oh, there you are, Fluffy," I said, forcing a cheerful

tone, though inside I was quaking. How had Mrs Emery known Syl was there? "I wondered where she'd got to."

I moved forward as if to take Syl from Mrs Emery, but the woman ignored me.

"Search the whole room," she said to the two bodyguards, and my heart sank. This was about to get extremely hard to bluff my way out of.

Sure enough, in a moment, one of the big guys was back, the real collar in his hand. Mrs Emery took it from him. Her face was hard as flint.

"I don't understand," Adrian said, his gaze darting from the collar to me and back again. "Where did that come from? And what's it got to do with the cat?"

"It's not a cat." Mrs Emery shook the spitting length of fur dangling from her hand, and it was as if Syl unfolded somehow, until her feet reached the floor, and she stood there, fully human and shocked out of her skin.

Adrian leapt back in horror. "It's a *shifter?*"

"Yes." With a nasty smile, Mrs Emery snapped the collar in her other hand around Syl's neck. "But not for long."

Dazed, Syl just stood there, as if she couldn't quite understand how she had come to be in human form. I didn't understand it myself—there was no way in the world that had been a voluntary shift, and how the *hell* had Mrs

Emery forced her into human form?—but I had more pressing concerns. I whipped the one throwing knife I had on me out of my boot and launched it straight at Mrs Emery, screaming for Jake at the top of my lungs.

Not even batting an eyelid, Mrs Emery held out her hand, palm facing the airborne blade in the universal sign for "stop", and the knife clattered to the floor mid-flight. Shit. That was the only weapon I had. Cocktail frocks weren't the best for disguising my usual array of blades.

The corporate types were still staring in shock, but the two bodyguards had leapt into action. One made a grab for me that only missed because I dropped to the floor and scrambled under the altar. Popping up on the other side, I shoulder-charged Irene, sending her flying into Bruno and Newton, and looked around for a weapon.

I found nothing, but fortunately Jake chose that moment to skid out of the side corridor, breathing hard. I'd been so focused I hadn't even heard the sound of him breaking out of his cell. He threw a blast of flame across the altar and I hit the deck again to avoid it.

Everyone else did the same, except for Newton, who wasn't fast enough, and caught it full in the face. He fell back, screaming in agony. The others scrambled to get out of his way as fire seared its way across his skin.

Adrian lunged across the floor and caught my leg in an iron grip. I twisted onto my back and took the greatest pleasure in driving my other foot straight between his legs. Lexi: one, gonads: nil. He let go abruptly and curled himself into an agonised ball.

The bodyguards were on the floor, too, cowering behind the altar so as to avoid becoming another human torch as Jake stalked forward, spraying the room with fire. Mrs Emery dragged Syl in front of her, using her as a human shield, and raised her free hand.

To my surprise, an answering fire burst forth from it. I'd been prepared for metalshaping, or a gust of wind, but fire? Where had that come from? Jake looked equally shocked, but he recovered quickly. Two great sheets of flame met in the middle of the room, and the heat and noise was unbelievable.

It even roused Apollo from his stupor. The god turned his head toward the sound, and I leapt up, remembering the key in my bra. This was my chance, while everyone was focused on the fire fight.

That lock on the back of his collar beckoned as I staggered to the altar, the key gripped tight in one fist. One of the bodyguards scuttled sideways under the altar when he saw me coming, and I knew I only had a moment. I rammed the key into the lock and twisted it violently as I felt strong arms close around my legs. For a moment I teetered, struggling to get the collar to open, then I lost my balance and hit the floor.

The guy grabbed my head and bashed it down on the hard dirt, making my ears ring. A white light burst above my head, and at first I thought I was seeing stars. But it was coming from Apollo. His discarded collar hurtled past and struck the wall with a metallic clang.

I jerked forward and slammed my head into the bridge of the guy's nose. Maybe he'd thought I'd go down easy because I was a girl. The look on his face as he reared back, blood pouring from his nostrils, was comical. I bucked him off, feeling the thrum of the god's power in my bones.

"The ring!" Apollo shouted, his voice strong now, commanding. He sat up on the altar, looking like a different person than the one who'd lain there waiting for death. He shone so bright I had to squint to look at him.

Mrs Emery cried out and directed a stream of fire at him, the muscles in her arms straining, as if she could physically force the flames onto her enemies. Jake only just managed to deflect it. Apparently, the god didn't have full access to his own powers without the ring, or surely the sun god could have blasted her out of existence for such an attack. I scrambled to my feet, looking around for it. Once he had it, Mrs Emery would be smeared all over this room.

She was shouting to her followers, though it was hard to hear over the roar of the flames. Wildly, I cast about for the ring. Where was it? It had been on the cushion, which Irene had taken off the altar, but the cushion now lay against the wall, kicked aside in the struggle. Where was the ring?

I spotted it at the same time that Irene did, and we both dove for it. She got there first and snatched it up. I punched her, snapping her head back, but she didn't let go. Instead, she glared at me, blood dripping from her nose, and blew into my face.

Her expression changed to a self-satisfied smirk as I was flung backwards by a massive gust of wind. It caught me completely by surprise, though of course it shouldn't have. Damn. This was not the moment for the Zephyrs to remember their stolen airshaping skills.

Encouraged by her success, Bruno and Adrian joined her, and suddenly Jake was in danger of being roasted in his own flames as a howling gale sprang up in the cellar, buffeting the fire toward him. I couldn't move, pinned against the wall by the power of their airshaping.

The god roared, the shackles that still gripped his ankles the only thing holding him in place against the wind's fury. His blonde hair streamed back from his head, scattering sparks of fire, but the effort of freeing his arms seemed to have exhausted his abilities. Their avatars held most of their powers when they were in human form, Adrian had said. If I couldn't get the ring off that bitch it looked like a stalemate.

Still pinned to the wall, I started crabbing my way

sideways around the room. If I could just reach Irene, I'd make her sorry she'd ever been born. Her face was blown up like a puffer fish and bright red with effort as she continued to blow her stolen winds at Jake. Maybe I'd get lucky and she'd hyperventilate and pass out.

Adrian saw me coming. Under cover of Mrs Emery's wall of flame, he darted to the side and picked up the god's discarded collar. Judging by the murderous look in his eyes, he meant to use it on me, but Mrs Emery shouted at him, and he threw the collar to her instead.

She caught it one-handed, without letting her flames die away. Syl stood at her side—or cowered, more like it—and I yelled at her to move, to do something. I could see what was about to happen. Mrs Emery had pulled the same stunt the night before. But Syl stood as if frozen. She hadn't moved since her forced shift, as if the shock of suddenly finding herself in human form had been too great to bear.

Once again, the collar flew through the air, like a guided missile seeking its target. At the last minute, Apollo saw it coming and put up his hands in a futile attempt to stop it, but even over the roar of the flames I heard the click as it snapped shut around his neck. His bright light died immediately, and the god slumped down in defeat.

It was almost a relief when someone hit me and I spiralled down into darkness.

16

I swear I was only out for a second, but when I opened my eyes I was on my feet, back to the wall, my head throbbing with the filthiest headache I'd ever experienced. Bruno supported me on one side and one of the bodyguards on the other. Apollo lay on the altar again, securely chained at hand and foot, and Syl stood on the other side of the room, her upper arm held in a firm grip by Adrian. Her eyes were wide with fear. She looked too stunned to put up much of a fight.

And where was Jake? In a sudden panic that I'd missed his execution, I glanced around and found him on the floor, handcuffed and apparently unconscious. Strange that they hadn't collared him again. Even if they only had two, they could have used the one around Syl's neck, since it was clear she wasn't going to give them any trouble. Were they that scared of shifters? Or had they done something else to Jake?

I hadn't seen how they'd managed to take him down. A sick terror gnawed at my gut as I stared at his pale face, the dark lashes stark against his ashen cheeks. Maybe he was already dead.

But no, his chest was still rising and falling. That was something, at least. But for how much longer? Already, Adrian was approaching the altar, bearing the sacrificial knife on its cushion. Nick Crawshaw took the cushion from him and offered it to Mrs Emery with a bow, his face alight with anticipation.

Come on, Syl, move! I implored her, pushing the thought at her with everything I had. But she didn't respond. Not exactly a surprise, since our link had only ever worked when she was in cat form, but I was getting desperate. Jake was down for the count, Syl was comatose with shock—and I was running out of ideas. We could all be dead in the next ten minutes. My heart raced, right on the edge of panic. Maybe if I started something, she'd join in.

I rammed my elbow into Bruno's side as hard as I could. Predictably, he let go of my arm, and I stomped on the foot of the guy on my other side. Unfortunately, he was made of sterner stuff—or maybe his boots were. We struggled for a moment, but he was stronger than me. Though I kicked out at him and it must have hurt, he still had me pinned against the wall in moments, using his heavier body to hold me there.

"What exactly are you trying to accomplish?" Mrs Emery asked in a bored voice, as if I was no more than a toddler throwing my toys around in a hissy fit. "Charles, you have my permission to use whatever force you deem necessary to subdue her if she tries anything else."

The bodyguard nodded, though his eyes never left my face. "My pleasure, ma'am."

His nose was swollen, possibly broken, from when I'd head-butted him during our tussle on the floor. He'd probably enjoy a bit of payback. He shoved me, just for the hell of it, then stepped back. I took a deep breath for the first time in a while, released from his weight, if not from his grip.

Bruno took a firm hold on my other elbow, giving me a dirty look at the same time. I wasn't going to win a popularity contest with these guys, that was for sure. I hurt, too—my head pounded, my back felt like a single mass of bruises, and nearly every muscle ached—but I couldn't give up. Even though the chance of any of us making it out of here alive was small, and shrinking all the time, I'd go down fighting.

Mrs Emery continued to study me with a puzzled frown. "Give it up, girl. You're only hurting yourself for nothing. Do you really think a little thing like you can succeed against us?"

Who the hell was she calling a little thing? She was a

goddamn midget. Without those heels she always wore, she wouldn't even come up to my shoulder. But her words reminded me of the mice that were still in the house above us, and I called them down. They might be little, but perhaps they could sow some mayhem, enough to give me another chance. It was surprising how many people were scared of mice.

"We are growing strong, and we'll be stronger still after tonight," she continued. "Soon we will reach the tipping point, and the world will change. Not that you'll be there to see it, of course, though you could have been if you'd learned to play nicely. Adrian says you're a Cybelean." She shook her head. "Such ingratitude."

"She said she was an Aristaean, too," Bruno said, shooting me a poisonous look, "but I checked with Gerald in Bourneville and he'd never heard of her. He rang me just now to confirm."

Mrs Emery's cold gaze swept over me searchingly, as if she could see inside my skin. "Well, there's something odd there, certainly, but it doesn't matter now."

I quailed, wondering what she had spotted. Her words reminded me uncannily of what Jake had said that first time I'd met him in the bookshop. *There are basically three kinds of people in the world: shapers, shifters, and sheep. You're not a shifter, and you're certainly not a shaper, but you don't feel like a sheep either. So what are you?* I could almost feel nostalgic for his arrogance now, but he, too, had sensed something odd about me. So I wasn't an Aristaean, and I was no closer to knowing what I was than before. Most likely, I would die here, never knowing where my strange abilities had come from.

Not that that was my biggest regret right now. I looked across at Syl. I'd brought such trouble into her life—some friend I'd been. She'd still be happily living in Crosston in the little apartment we'd so briefly shared if it wasn't for me. And Jake. I'd never got to know him better, or done any of the things I had occasionally fantasised about doing to that cute shaper body of his.

Okay, maybe more than occasionally.

He still lay unmoving, and my heart clenched at how vulnerable he looked. He'd tried so hard to save his god— his god who now lay chained, his blue eyes fixed on me as if hoping for some eleventh-hour reprieve.

Sorry, buddy, I'm all out of ideas.

The mice were on their way, but I was really stretching for a way to use them effectively. Mrs Emery didn't strike me as the type to leap shrieking behind the nearest man at the sight of a mouse.

Crawshaw shifted impatiently, eyeing the knife on its cushion, but Mrs Emery wasn't done with the lecture yet.

"You're clearly a traitor to humanity, and there will be no room in our new world for shaper and shifter lovers."

She shot a glance filled with loathing at Syl. "Filthy beasts. The world belongs to humans, and we will wipe the rest of this scum—and their gods—from the face of the earth."

"But not before taking our power for yourselves," Apollo said. His voice had lost that authority that had reverberated in my bones now that he wore the collar again, but at least he seemed more alert now.

"No," she agreed, in a voice that was poisonously sweet. "Not before taking your power for ourselves."

"It will destroy you. Your mortal bodies were never meant to handle such stresses."

"Not shared amongst so many," Mrs Emery said. "In a society of equals, there will be many who enjoy such power, rather than the oligopoly the shapers have created."

Did any of them really believe this crap? I gazed around at the faces of the corporate clones. They were all rapt attention, despite the fact they'd probably heard this speech many times before. Maybe that was how they justified the slaughter to themselves. Perhaps they'd started out filled with idealistic zeal for a new, more equal world.

Except this cellar was awfully empty if that rhetoric was true. Hell, there'd been more people here the night before to share in the powers of the god of the west wind, and he was small potatoes compared to the power they would harvest from Apollo. Where were the multitudes waiting to share in this bonanza?

Shouldered out of the way by the elite, that's where. If they'd ever believed in that ideal, they certainly didn't anymore. The handful of people here would take all of Apollo's power to themselves, elevating themselves to the status, surely, of minor gods. It would be nice if Apollo was right and they couldn't handle the power, but I had the feeling Mrs Emery knew what she was doing. There were just enough here to suit her purposes, and no more.

Apparently, the time for declaiming was over. Mrs Emery finally took pity on Crawshaw, who was practically salivating at her side, and reached for the ceremonial dagger. Damn, but that thing looked sharp. I swallowed hard as bile burned the back of my throat, knowing what was coming.

As she picked up the dagger, her silver cuff caught the light of the flickering torches. It had the same sort of decorative swirls on it as the collar around Apollo's neck. Maybe it was made of the same strange metal, but it didn't seem to stop Mrs Emery accessing her powers, unfortunately.

Apollo closed his brilliant blue eyes, his outstretched arms taut with tension. I wanted to close mine, too, so I didn't have to see that dagger fall, see the bright arterial blood spurting as she slashed his throat, but I forced myself to keep looking. If he opened his eyes again, I wanted him to know that I was here for him—that at least someone cared, even if there was nothing else I could do for him.

Or was there?

"You're going to spend the rest of your lives looking over your shoulders." I had to keep her talking, just for a few more moments. At the same time, I sent my awareness questing out as far as I could, further than I ever had before. "Every time you use their stolen magic, you'll be wondering when the gods will make you pay the price for these murders."

Mrs Emery's lip curled in a sneer. "The gods are all too busy running and cowering, wondering if they will be next. They don't care who I kill, as long as it isn't them."

"Hades cares." He'd tried so hard to stop me bringing the ring here. He'd sent that enormous hulking brute of his to stop us, and I'd touched its strange dark mind. I'd never felt anything like it before. Now I strained, not quite sure how I was doing it, but seeking that strangeness again. The effort felt as if it would split my aching head apart.

The sneer turned into a full-on laugh. "Hades has spent his whole life lurking in the shadows. Nothing could tempt him to risk his precious skin." She stepped forward, knife in hand. With her free hand, she stroked Apollo's lank hair, almost caressing it. The god shuddered at her touch.

I shuddered too—or was that the ground? The packed earth floor vibrated beneath my feet. Mrs Emery looked around, uncertain, then shrugged and took a firm hold of Apollo's hair. She laid the glinting blade against his throat, ready for the slice that would end his life.

And then the cellar floor exploded. Clods of earth flew through the air, spraying the room with dirt. The ground shifted alarmingly, making me stagger. With a noise like a freight train roaring through the station, a giant three-headed dog leapt up onto the altar, straddling the trembling god.

The cavalry had arrived.

❧

I never thought I'd be so glad to see Cerberus again. His snake-like tail wagged ever so slightly as his glowing red eyes met mine. I could hardly believe I'd managed to call him.

Mrs Emery leapt back with a shriek, but she was too slow. The middle head swooped down, fast as a snake striking, and bit off her arm. The ceremonial dagger hit the floor as blood spurted from the stump. She stared at it, shocked into silence. Time seemed to stand still as her face drained of colour, then her eyes closed and she sagged to the floor in a graceless heap.

Her collapse released pandemonium in the cellar. A chorus of screams rose as Cerberus leapt down off the altar, landing with a thud that shook the room again. People scattered as the left head snapped at Bruno, who released my arm and fled back through the archway towards the exit. The right head lunged at Adrian, who backed away so fast he tripped over Mrs Emery and sprawled across the earthen floor. He kept his wits about him and rolled fast enough to evade those great jaws. Cerberus's teeth caught his jacket, but Adrian managed to wriggle out of it and scramble to a temporary safety down the corridor that led to the cells.

The bodyguard dragged me in front of him and started backing rapidly for the archway in Bruno's wake, as if my body could shield him from the giant dog. I didn't approve of this plan, so I elbowed him hard enough in the gut to make him let go, and staggered free. Syl caught me and stopped me from falling. My head throbbed, and the dizziness was worse than I'd thought now that I was moving again. The bodyguard disappeared into the darkness, but I didn't care. I had the feeling he hadn't gone for reinforcements. No one would be mad enough to take on Hades' hell hound.

"Are you all right?" Syl shouted above the groaning of timbers and Irene's constant, high-pitched screams. "You're pretty banged up."

"I'll live."

Maybe. The odds had certainly improved, but another tremor shook the room, and bits of dirt and brick dust fell like grubby rain from above. Had Cerberus saved us from being sacrificed only to bring the house down on our heads? The hole he had appeared from was enormous, and the far wall of the room teetered right on the edge of it. The wall began to bulge as the bottom row of bricks succumbed to the pressure. First one brick, then another, dropped into the hole. If that wall was loadbearing, we were in serious trouble.

Through it all, Irene kept up a constant screaming that pierced my aching head like a smoke alarm going off. She was trapped in the corner, cut off from either exit by Cerberus's great bulk. Personally, I would have kept my trap shut and hoped he didn't notice me, but perhaps there was no actual thought process going on behind those wide eyes. You'd think that people who messed with gods might have been at least a little prepared to meet some divine opposition, but apparently it hadn't occurred to any of them that the gods might fight back, and that some of them had some pretty mean allies.

All three heads swung to face the screaming woman, growling louder than a thunderstorm. The middle one, which had chowed down on Mrs Emery's arm, dripped blood and saliva in disturbing quantities. All three had a hungry look, and Irene's screaming suddenly ended in a tearful little hiccup as the massive animal took a threatening step closer.

"Cerberus!" Apollo was covered in dust and, it must be said, what looked like half a bucket of dog drool. He shook his chained arms at the beast. "Quickly, boy!"

Jake stirred and levered himself up onto one elbow, as if

the sound of his god's voice had roused him. He looked worse than I felt, covered in brick dust and blood, tufts of hair sticking up at wild angles.

I tried to go to him, but I wasn't moving so well myself, and Syl had to catch me before I went down. The head injury was bothering me more and more, and there was a roaring in my ears that had nothing to do with the chaos in the cellar. I shook my head to try to clear them and nearly passed out again.

The floor shuddered as Cerberus bounded back to the altar. Two heads took a chain each, while the third licked Apollo's face with a tongue as long as my arm. He didn't look too pleased by the affection. With a sound like someone shaking a tin full of nails, Cerberus chomped through the chains, freeing the god's arms.

"Girl!" He gestured imperiously at me. "Where is the key for this abomination?"

He tugged at the collar around his neck, unconsciously mimicking Jake's fretful movements when I'd seen him in his cell. Jake was on his feet now, swaying perilously close to the gaping hole in the ground. Frankly, I was more concerned about him falling to his death than I was with the god's freedom.

"I don't know." I hadn't seen it since the bodyguard had crash-tackled me. I'd kept my grip on it then, but when I woke from being knocked out, it was gone. Someone had taken it while I was out, but where was it now? "Syl, who took it?"

She gave a helpless shrug. "That guy who was holding you."

I didn't know which one she meant, but it didn't matter, since they'd both fled. Damn. That was awkward.

Cerberus moved to the foot of the altar and began worrying at the shackles that bound Apollo's legs. Apollo tugged impatiently at them until Cerberus growled at him. I felt the growl deep in my chest, reverberating, and the foundations quivered in sympathy. More dust fell on our heads and the joists holding up the floor above us creaked alarmingly. Cerberus bit through the last links in the chain and Apollo hopped off the altar with alacrity.

At the edge of the pit, he caught Jake's arm. Another brick toppled in and an ominous rumble began beneath our feet.

"Let's get out of here before this whole place collapses." Still holding Jake's arm, he leapt into the yawning hole.

I gaped at him—or rather, at the hole he'd disappeared into. Seriously? He expected us to go down there? Longingly, I glanced back through the archway, towards the outside world, but going that way meant facing a swarm of irate shadow shapers.

"What about the ring?" I shouted to Syl over the groaning of the timbers overhead and a noise like a large truck approaching.

"Forget it," she shouted back, as one brick after another toppled into the pit, until, with a sudden rush, the whole wall subsided. The archway behind began a slow collapse, and the joist above my head cracked with a sound like a gun going off. Syl held out her hand to me. "Jump!"

I grabbed it and together we leapt into the darkness.

17

I screamed all the way down, too. I was normally pretty good with heights, but this was something else. I left my stomach far behind as we fell, the only sensation the wind rushing past my body, and the feel of Syl's warm hand still clutched in mine. There was no way I was letting go, either. In the utter blackness of that place, it seemed that, unless I held on tight, we might each fall forever, separated in an endless descent.

I could hardly tell whether my eyes were open or closed. It made no difference either way to the punishing darkness that pressed in on us. In the first moments I'd been able to see the faint light from the cellar above, brick dust drifting against the light as the roaring of the building's collapse chased us down the unnatural shaft. But after a moment, it had been as if someone flicked a switch, and the light and the noise disappeared, so there was only the endless falling. Well, that, and my screaming.

It felt as though I'd been falling for an hour, and I'd screamed myself hoarse, when suddenly we stopped. There was no pain, and it took a moment before I realised we actually had stopped, and I lay on a firm, cool surface. More than a little surprised to find I hadn't been smashed to smithereens all over the floor, I lay there a moment, panting and getting used to the idea that I wasn't about to die after all.

Syl's hand squeezed mine in the dark. "Well, that was fun. *Not*. I think I've lost the hearing in my right ear."

I squeezed back and sat up cautiously, setting my aching head spinning. It was still pitch black and I had no idea where we were. "Sorry. Where the hell are we?"

"Got it in one, my dear," said a voice I knew.

"Alberto!" Gratefully, I turned toward the sound. "Don't you have any lights in this joint?"

"Ah." He sounded a little embarrassed. "I keep forgetting you're human." He snapped his fingers and the world flooded with light, though there was no obvious light source. The soft glow showed the strangest scene.

I was sitting on a paved area in front of a house that looked like it had been lifted straight from a historical romance. Or rather, not a house, but a mansion—some lord's massive country estate. Gargoyles peered down from a roof that towered way above us. The columns that held up the portico were taller than the trees lining the drive behind us. I almost expected to see a carriage and four come sweeping around the graceful curves of the drive and across the little stream that slid silently under the bridge. It was that kind of a house.

Behind it, the gentle folds of low hills rose, covered in grey-green grass and small copses of trees. I stood up, overwhelmed by the size of the building. It must have taken an army of servants to keep a place like this running, but there was no sign of them. Apollo and Jake were sitting on the first of the wide steps that led up to the grand entrance, the god supporting the fireshaper, who didn't look any better than when I'd last glimpsed him in the cellar, though someone had removed his handcuffs, at least. For a guy with so much power, Jake always seemed to end up more damaged than anyone else in our little adventures. My heart lifted, though, to see him there, beaten but still alive.

Cerberus stood wagging next to his master. If that *was* his master.

"Alberto?" I said again, uncertain now.

The man standing next to the giant dog looked nothing like the Alberto I knew. He was short and stocky, perhaps sixty, with greying hair cut short and clear blue eyes in a weathered brown face.

"Yes." He smiled and a web of crow's feet appeared around his eyes. Was this his real appearance, or another disguise he shrugged on when it suited him? He looked like a farmer who'd spent his whole life outdoors squinting into the sun, not the Lord of the Underworld. "Welcome to my humble abode."

Syl snorted. "I suppose it's not bad for a little place, but I'd expected something a little more … I don't know— Greek?"

"It's got Doric columns," he pointed out, then laughed. "Oh, don't look at me like that. You can't blame a man for remodelling every now and then. Anything starts to look tired after a few centuries."

"It's certainly imposing," I said. Personally, I'd expected the décor in the underworld to be a little more tortured. Black marble, maybe, with lots of screaming faces and jets of fire. Maybe that got boring, too, after a while. The country estate certainly made for a more soothing afterlife, and it seemed to fit with the face he wore. "We're not actually dead, though, are we? I mean, it looks very nice and all, but I don't want to stay here permanently."

Greek myths were full of stories about how hard it was to get in and out of the underworld. It would be too bad if we'd escaped the debacle in the cellar only to end up trapped in the afterlife.

Hades pouted. I couldn't think of him as Alberto while he wore this other form. His voice was the only thing about him that I recognised. "You've only just arrived, and already you're thinking of leaving?"

"Nothing personal. It just seems like an important point to be clear on."

"Don't worry. You're my special guests, and no harm will come to you while you're here."

That sounded great, but I made a mental note not to eat any pomegranate seeds during our stay. That hadn't turned out so well for poor Persephone.

"And you've brought my nephew," he added. "For that alone, you deserve to be richly rewarded."

"It might have been a more impressive rescue if they'd managed to get this collar off me first," Apollo said, running his finger under the evil thing and shooting me a black look. Ungrateful bastard.

"Never mind," Hades said. "Come inside and we'll have a look at it. I'm sure we'll be able to figure something out."

"Syl's got one too," I said.

"I can't—I can't shift," she said, her voice revealing the panic lurking just beneath the surface.

He gave her a sympathetic look, but all he said was: "Interesting." Then he waved us before him up the steps. Apollo strode ahead, leaving Jake sitting on the step.

I stopped at his side. "Need a hand?"

He looked like he would have liked to say no, but then he sighed and reached for my outstretched hand. "I swear, one day, I'm going to spend twenty-four hours with you where no one is trying to kill us."

"It's your own fault," I said. "My life was quiet until you came into it. You might want to rethink the whole hanging-out-with-gods thing."

He shot me a sideways glance full of laughter as I hauled him to his feet. "Says the girl whose favourite drinking buddy is Lord of the Underworld."

"That's different," I protested. "I didn't know he was a god. You knew what you were getting into when you went chasing after Apollo."

"And just as well he did," Hades said, coming through the door behind us, "or Apollo would be toast."

The country manor theme continued in the foyer, which was panelled in dark wood and hung with a whole gallery of grim-looking portraits. Cerberus plonked himself down on the red patterned carpet and began scratching behind one ear vigorously.

"He doesn't seem particularly grateful." I glared at the back of Apollo's blonde head. He was contemplating one of the portraits, a painting of an older man with a full, grey beard and a stern expression on his face.

"He'll get over it," Hades said. "He's just ticked about the collar."

"I can hear you, you know," Apollo said without turning around. "I wish Zeus were here. He'd blast this filthy thing out of existence."

"And probably blast your head with it," Hades said

230

tartly. "Your father has many fine qualities, but finesse isn't one of them. Always going at things like a bull at a gate."

"Can we ask him to help?" I butted in, before a full-scale family argument erupted. Was the greybeard in the painting Zeus? I guess I could see a resemblance between him and the grey-haired Hades. If I remembered my Greek mythology correctly, Hades was Zeus's brother, which made him Apollo's uncle.

"Sadly, no. That friend I told you about, the night you left Berkley's Bay to save Holly? The one who disappeared, that we occasionally receive cryptic messages from? That's Zeus."

Oh. I figured he'd meant Apollo. How many of the gods were missing? Seemed like the First Shapers were in a lot more trouble than I'd imagined, if someone had managed to take out the father of the gods.

"You'd think the god of electricity would be able to manage a decent email," Hades continued. "A text, even! But no. He can't even string a coherent sentence together. All we get are these almost random words popping up on computer screens, or even TVs."

Whoa. Like the cat food commercial and BEWARE RING? That was Zeus? Come to think of it, that alarm clock worked on electricity, too.

"I think he helped me," I said. Apollo gave me an impatient glance, as if wondering why any god would bother with a lowlife like me. "Someone gave me the combination to Mrs Emery's safe—the numbers appeared on the clock radio in my room. That wasn't you?"

Apollo rolled his eyes and indicated the collar. "No power here, sweetheart, remember?"

Sweetheart? I was getting sorrier by the minute that we'd rescued him.

"Besides, electricity's not my thing."

"I can't believe you managed to lose the father of the gods. How long has he been missing?"

Hades snorted. "We didn't *lose* him. It's not like I put him down somewhere and now I can't remember where I left him. He just disappeared. All we've had since Hephaistos died are these odd, cryptic messages."

"Are you sure they're even from him?" Maybe Zeus was dead, too, though I didn't want to suggest that to his brother and son.

"Pretty sure. He hasn't arrived in the underworld, so I know he's still alive, but he wouldn't be away so long unless someone or something was preventing him from returning. I don't know who else would be trying to communicate with us in this way."

"Then to find him you need to know who took him. Presumably, it was the same person who took Apollo. Mrs Emery?"

Apollo shrugged. "I don't know who did it."

"What do you mean, you don't know?" The guy was an airhead.

"I mean I went to sleep in my own bed one night, and the next thing I remember is waking up in a cell with this damn collar on and no ring. I have no idea how I got there."

Okay, that was weird. That was two of us with screwy memories, though my case was different to the god's. Still, I'd rather imagine that someone was playing mind games with both of us than believe I was going crazy.

Hades frowned, and we all stared at Apollo, who glared back as if the whole mess was somehow our fault. "And now my ring's probably buried under a ton of rubble, thanks to Cerberus."

Cerberus's ears twitched at the sound of his name, and Apollo sighed.

"Not that I'm not grateful to be rescued, of course." He flicked a rather shamefaced glance at his uncle, as if belatedly realising how ungracious he sounded. "It just makes me twitchy to be without my avatar. Anything could happen to it."

"Actually …" Syl said, reaching into her pocket. "Catch!"

She tossed something small to Apollo, something that glinted gold as it spun in a graceful arc.

Apollo snatched it out of the air, his face lighting up with real joy. "My ring!"

"I grabbed it during the fighting," Syl said. So she hadn't been completely out of it after all. Maybe some of her shock had been an act to turn attention away from herself.

Apollo slid the ring onto the little finger of his left hand. "Thank you. If there's anything I can ever do for you …"

Cerberus coughed, a deep, hacking sound.

Hades flicked him a distracted glance. "Have you been eating grass again?"

Cerberus gazed at his master almost apologetically, and coughed again. It was the middle head coughing, and the other two stared at the carpet between his massive paws, as if pretending they had nothing whatsoever to do with what was happening.

"Cerberus!" There was a warning note in Hades' voice, and the two outer heads hung lower as the dog's stomach convulsed.

"He looks like he's trying to bring up a fur ball," Syl murmured.

The dog heaved and hacked again.

"Cerberus! Outside!"

But it was too late. In a rush of stinking dog vomit, Mrs Emery's arm reappeared, the cuff still gleaming on its wrist. Cerberus's tail thumped weakly against the floor as all three heads gave Hades a guilty look.

Hades sighed. "Bad dog! Not the carpet *again*."

18

I didn't see Syl again until the next day—if you could call it a day when you were someplace outside the real-world universe. I asked Jake where the underworld was located, but he just shrugged and told me not to be so literal. At any rate, it got dark, then it got light again, so I was calling it a new day. I spent most of it either sleeping or roaming the echoing halls of Hades' mansion, and the daylight was leaching from the sky again when I found Syl. She was curled up on a lounge in a little paved courtyard where a fountain splashed water into a pool full of slow-moving koi.

She'd gone off with Hades and Apollo the night before, eager to have her collar removed. All day, I'd been waiting to hear the result. She was curled around herself as if something hurt—or as if she was trying to curl up the way her cat self would have done. My heart ached to see she still wore the collar. It was probably both.

I dragged a chair over and sat down, not sure what to say. Her hair was in its usual long, dark plait down her back, and she wore a black singlet and black jeans. The dull silver gleam of the collar around her neck made her look like some exotic goth. I hated the thing, but there was no denying it was beautiful.

"Did Hades figure out if the scrollwork on the collar means anything?" Clearly there was no point asking if he'd worked out a way to get it off.

She shrugged, a tiny movement of one bare shoulder. She didn't look at me, or even open her eyes. Lying there, curled so tightly around her pain, she looked smaller than I remembered. Even as a cat, Syl's personality could fill a room. Now, it was as if all the life and colour had drained out of her, leaving only a husk behind.

"So what's the next move?" Surely Hades and Apollo, with all their combined wisdom, could find a way to remove a couple of stupid collars. "There must be something else he can try, right?"

She didn't even shrug this time, just unfolded in a fluid move that was very catlike and stalked inside. My eyes stung with tears as I watched her go. All the times I'd harassed her lately over refusing to take human form came back to slam me with guilt. Now she was stuck this way—maybe forever. How would she cope?

I had to find a way to fix this.

I sat in the courtyard until the sky darkened completely, the splash of the fountain soothing my guilty heart. No stars shone overhead, but the night wasn't completely dark. A faint silvery light sparkled on the fountain and lit the manicured curves of the shrubs lining the courtyard walls.

Eventually, I heard footsteps echoing on marble floors, and the sound of male voices approaching. The light levels rose as if in greeting as the Lord of the Underworld stepped out into the courtyard, closely followed by Jake.

"The house told me you were here," Hades said. "Have you spoken to Syl?"

"Not really. I mean, I spoke, but she didn't answer. Wouldn't talk to me at all." Sudden hope surged in my heart. "Why? Have you found a way to get the collars off?"

"No."

Hades looked tired, and I wondered if he'd had any sleep since we arrived. Then I wondered if gods even needed sleep. At least Jake looked better.

"Any clues at least?"

"Not a one. I've tried everything I could think of—I even tried forcing a change on Syl, which is something any god should be able to do, thinking she could just slip out of the damn thing. But it blocks my power even though I'm not the one wearing it. Just seems to soak up anything I can throw at it." He sighed. "Apollo's beside himself, and Syl won't come out of her room. I was hoping you could talk to her."

"I don't think she wants to talk. She's too spooked by this whole thing." I looked at Jake. "You're a metalshaper. Can't you make a key?" He'd changed a random key so it would start the car we stole in Crosston—surely this would be easy for him.

"Tried that. Nothing I made would open them. There's some kind of protection on the collars that seems to repel shaping."

"What about the cuff, then?"

"What about it?"

"If the cuff controls the collars, maybe you can use that."

Hades snorted. "Maybe I could, if I was prepared to put it on—but that's not a risk I'm willing to take. For all we know, it only works for the Emery woman. I could find myself just as trapped as Syl and Apollo."

"Besides, we're only speculating that it controls them," Jake said, dropping onto the lounge that Syl had vacated and stretching his long legs out in front of him. "It may have some other purpose."

"They look the same," I objected.

"They're definitely made of the same substance, and probably by the same person," Jake said, "but that doesn't prove the cuff controls the collars. It could just be some kind of protective talisman."

"If so, it didn't work very well, did it?" That gave me a certain grim satisfaction. I wouldn't be shedding any tears for Mrs Emery.

Hades sat on the stone coping around the fountain and trailed his hand in the water. "I'm not giving up, but I'll need to think on it for a while. Once Apollo stops throwing tantrums and sets his mind to the problem, we're bound to come up with something." Was he trying to reassure me or himself? He didn't sound all that convinced. "Of course, you're welcome to stay here until we do, if you wish."

"Thank you." I was quite sure Syl wouldn't budge from this place while that thing was still around her neck, but the urge to get out there and *do* something to fix this disaster was eating at me.

Jake looked at me as if he could tell what I was thinking. "If only there was something you could steal that would help. Your talents in that area are certainly impressive. Apollo had better make sure he keeps an eye on that ring of his."

I felt my face heating, and was glad of the low lighting. Obviously, the fact that I'd had no trouble stealing it from *him* still rankled.

"Why did you take it, by the way, if it wasn't to give to the shadow shapers? You never did tell me."

Despite all we'd been through, the habit of protecting my secret was still strong, so I settled for a half-truth. "I thought I recognised the ring, but I couldn't remember why it seemed so familiar. I wanted to show it to my mother."

He raised an eyebrow. "And what did she say?"

Frustration welled up inside me. "I couldn't find her."

And then the whole thing poured out—how everything in my mother's house had been the same, but another woman had been living there, how I couldn't find anyone else I remembered either—even how the records of my own existence had vanished.

"That's bizarre," Jake said when I'd finished. "Not a single person? What about other family? Your father?"

"He took off when I was still a kid."

"Siblings?"

"I had a brother, but he's dead."

His eyes softened. "I'm sorry. What was his name?"

I opened my mouth—but nothing came out. His name—what was his name? I could picture his face, but I ransacked my memories and came up empty-handed. Panic began to bubble deep inside me. I *couldn't* have forgotten my own brother's name. I glanced wildly between Jake and Hades. Jake's brow was creased with concern, but I couldn't quite put a name to the expression in Hades' eyes.

"I—I can't remember." I shook my head, horrified with myself. "What's the matter with me?"

"That's ... an odd thing to forget," Jake said. "What *do* you remember about him?"

I clasped my hands together in my lap to hide their shaking. "He was two years older than me, about my height. He gave me a bow for my fourteenth birthday and taught me to use it. He had blue eyes, darker than yours, and blonde hair. Everyone liked him. He died trying to protect me from a mob."

"What else?"

"When I started high school, he beat up Antonio Estevez for calling me ugly and making me cry." I stopped and he motioned me to continue. I shook my head helplessly, the moment stretching on and on. There must be more! "That's all I can remember."

"That's it? That's like a highlights reel." Concern shadowed his blue eyes. "What about the rest of it? What was his favourite colour? What were his hobbies? Who was his best friend? Where did he work? What was his first girlfriend's name?"

I held up my hands, close to tears. "I don't *know*. I don't remember any of this."

He leaned in, his stare intense. "This isn't right. Someone's been messing with your head."

"But why? I'm no one special."

"Aren't you? How can you be sure? I could feel there was something different about you the moment I met you. That's why I thought you were a shadow shaper. That knack of yours for controlling animals seemed like the kind of thing a shadow shaper would be able to do." I opened my mouth to protest, but he shushed me with a smile.

"Don't bother pretending you don't know what I'm talking about. I think the cat's well and truly out of the bag as far as your abilities go. And for what it's worth, I'm sorry for ever believing that you were a shadow shaper."

"Apology accepted," I said after a long moment. Jake's on-again, off-again hostility hardly seemed important any more. Could my life possibly get any more screwed up?

Hades cleared his throat. "I'm sorry for your problems, but I think our main focus at the moment has to be the collars."

"Of course." I couldn't see what anyone could do to help me anyway, and it was more important to free Syl and Apollo. I stood abruptly. "I think I'll turn in. It's been a pretty shitty day."

They both said goodnight, and I went back to the palatial room I'd been assigned, and sank into the welcoming softness of the massive ebony bed. It took me a long time to go to sleep, but just before I drifted off, it occurred to me that that odd expression on Hades' face had looked a lot like guilt.

❦

I wandered the forest paths behind Hades' mansion, unnerved by the quiet. No birdsong broke the stillness, no small animals rustled in the undergrowth. There wasn't even any wind to stir the leaves above my head. Though in every other way the little wood was exactly the same as a real one, even down to the sunlight slanting through the trees, the silence was so unnatural it made my skin crawl.

Through force of habit, I reached out with my mind, but I found an empty landscape. No bright sparks of animal life hidden among the trees. That was unnatural, too. Well, it *was* the land of the dead.

Knowing that didn't stop me feeling weirded out. I burst out of the trees onto the open lawn at the back of the house, breathing harder than I should. The only animal life in the whole place lumbered toward me across the grass, a branch as thick as my arm and taller than I was clenched firmly in three sets of teeth.

I walked to meet him, grateful for his living presence. I'd been alone with my thoughts for too long. He dropped the branch on the grass at my feet. Three giant pink tongues lolled out of three enormous mouths as he watched me expectantly.

"You can't be serious," I said. "You expect me to throw that?"

His dark eyes glittered as if red flames leapt in their depths. All six of them looked from me down to the branch, then back at me.

THROW STICK.

"That's not a stick. It's a goddamn tree trunk. I could probably just about lift it, but throw it? Not a chance, buster."

His tail continued to wag hopefully. *THROW STICK,* he insisted.

I patted the nearest head then kept walking, heading back toward the house. After a moment, Cerberus picked up the branch and trotted after me. He'd been following me around ever since I'd arrived, as if fascinated by the only person who could command him, apart from his master. At least he'd forgiven me for putting him to sleep that time on the road.

"Shouldn't you be guarding the gates of Hell or something?"

He wagged but said nothing. Maybe Hades had a more modern system in place these days. Electric fences, perhaps. I'd have asked him but I'd barely seen him since our chat in the courtyard. He and Apollo and Syl had been closeted away together, and I'd been left with my own unhappy thoughts.

Jake appeared on the terrace, a mug in his hand. When I was close enough, I could smell the delicious aroma of coffee. "You're up early," he said, blue eyes watching me over the rim of his mug. "Couldn't you sleep?"

"I slept fine. Just feeling restless."

And frustrated. I was no closer to finding out where my mysterious power had come from, or why Apollo's stupid ring felt like it was trying to talk to me, or what the hell had happened to my mother and everyone else I remembered from my home town, if they even existed. My dead brother appeared to be a not-very-good figment of my imagination. Even *I* didn't exist, according to the official records. Basically, I had a whole bunch of ugly questions and not a single good answer—and I really didn't want to talk about it. Bad enough that I'd been thinking about it non-stop.

"How about you?" I asked. "You look a lot better today."

"I feel great. Slept like the dead."

"Well, this is definitely the right place for that."

He grinned, and I couldn't help smiling back. Damn, but he was cute—especially now that he was cleaned up and didn't look like he was about to pass out. For once, no one was trying to kill us, so I boosted myself up onto the stone balustrade next to him and took a moment to appreciate what a fine physical specimen he was. His shoulder brushed against mine and I breathed in his familiar smoky scent, wondering how it would feel to brush a few more body parts together.

"It's a nice quiet spot for a little break." He shook his head. "All those years everyone thought Alberto was sleeping the day away in the cellar, and all the time he was sneaking off here."

"It's a little too quiet for my taste." I kind of wished he'd stop talking. He was interrupting a perfectly good fantasy.

"Oh?" He arched an eyebrow. "You live in Berkley's Bay. I thought you liked quiet."

Cerberus dropped his branch with a thud and stared expectantly at us. I sighed. Looked like the fantasy would have to wait. "He wants you to throw the stick," I said.

"Big stick."

"Yeah, that's what I said."

Jake set his mug down on the balustrade and lightly vaulted over it. He hefted the stick like a spear, the muscles of his arm bulging. Nice. "Zeus's balls. This thing is heavy."

Cerberus's ears pricked in anticipation. Jake hurled the stick, grunting with effort. It barely travelled any distance at all, and Cerberus flopped down with a disgusted groan.

I burst out laughing. "I don't think he's impressed."

Jake marched across the grass and picked it up again.

"Try to put some effort into it this time," I said.

He gave me a black look, then lifted the branch above his head. Flames burst from one end, and it took off like a rocket, zooming across the lawn all the way to the edge of the woods. Cerberus leapt up with a joyful bark and loped after it.

"Better?"

"Much. Although now he'll expect you to keep doing it all morning."

"Lucky I like dogs."

"He's not your average dog, though. Look what he did to Joe's truck."

"Are you worried about that? Don't be—I'll buy him a new one."

Cerberus dropped the branch at Jake's feet in triumph and Jake obligingly sent it whizzing across the lawn again.

Actually, I hadn't given poor Joe's truck another thought—I had much bigger things to worry about. "That's kind of you."

"Not really. I'll do anything to get you to finally agree to go on a date with me."

"What do you mean, *finally agree*?" I kept my tone as light and joking as his, but my heart began knocking against my ribs. My libido sat up and took notice, too. "When did you ever ask me to go on a date with you?"

Cerberus brought the branch back and Jake sent it off again, though it was starting to look a little shorter. If the game kept going much longer, the whole thing would be burned away.

"I *begged* you to go to lunch with me the day after we found those boys. You practically spat in my face."

"Yeah, well, if you go around threatening to set people's bookshops on fire, you've got to expect that there might be some social consequences." I fought to keep a silly grin off my face. Standing there with the fake sunlight shining on his dark head, blue eyes lit with amusement, he was all but irresistible. The guy sure knew how to turn on the charm. He threw Cerberus's stick again, and the muscles in his shoulders and arms did that awesome rippling thing. Damn, I could watch that all day. Syl had accused me of practically climbing into his lap that time he'd kissed me in the car, but who wouldn't? That was an experience I'd be very happy to explore further. A lot further.

Syl. Some of my enthusiasm faded. I'd never seen her so miserable, not even when we first fled Crosston together after the fire. What was a shifter who couldn't shift?

"Have you seen Hades and Apollo this morning?"

He glanced sharply at me, sensing my change in mood. "Hades said he still has a few things he can try. He hasn't given up hope yet."

"But Apollo has, right?"

The sun god's face had grown blacker and blacker as each new attempt to get the magical collar off his neck proved fruitless. Hades had even tried getting Cerberus to bite through it. I'd seen what those teeth could do to metal before, but he hadn't even scratched the silver collar. It clearly wasn't made of any ordinary metal.

"Apollo's been in captivity for a year. He's not in a good place right now. To come so close to freedom and essentially still be a prisoner …"

I could see how that would be hard for someone used to the powers of a god. "You're a metalshaper. What do you think? There must be some way to get the collars off."

Jake threw the stick, now barely half its original length, for Cerberus, then sat on the balustrade next to me, reclaiming his mug of coffee. "Zeus could probably do it—

but no one knows where he is. If Hephaistos was still alive, he could do it for sure. There was nothing he couldn't do with metal. But without either of them, or the right key, I don't know."

"Damn. I was hoping you might have had some brilliant idea. I'm worried about Syl. We might never get her out of here if we can't get that collar off." It was Syl's nature to hide from her troubles, and she'd never had a trouble as big as this one, that cut to the very heart of her existence. I had to fix this for her. My own problems could wait. "Didn't Hephaistos leave any notes on his work? Did he have a library or something?"

"If you mean, did he write down all his secrets for posterity, I'd be surprised. Gods don't like to share, and they have trouble imagining that they might ever cease to exist, so posterity never really comes into their thinking. Besides, a smith's expertise is practical. His magic was in his forge, not in words."

"So we either have to find Zeus, or hope that there might be some clue left in Hephaistos's smithy that can help us." Neither of those options sounded easy. "Do you know where it is?"

"Hephaistos's smithy? No, but Hades probably does."

I smiled brightly at him. "In that case, I'd love to go on a date with you."

He took my hand in his, but there was suspicion in those

blue eyes. "You would? Why do I have the feeling that I'm going to get shot at or beaten up again?" He stroked his thumb along my fingers and I tried to ignore the delicious sensations this produced.

"It's not my fault if you fireshapers are delicate."

Cerberus flopped down on the grass at our feet and proceeded to gnaw what was left of his stick into splinters. I rubbed his broad back with one foot, looking down at my fingers entwined with Jake's. Despite the problems that faced us, I felt a surge of happiness.

"You're a very determined woman, Lexi Jardine. Has anyone ever told you that?"

"All the time. You'll get used to it. So ... Hephaistos's smithy?"

He grinned. "It's a date."

THE END

Don't miss the next book, coming soon! For news on its release, plus special deals and other book news, sign up for my newsletter at www.marinafinlayson.com.

Reviews and word of mouth are vital for any author's success. If you enjoyed *Murdered Gods*, please take a moment to leave a short review where you bought it. Just a few words sharing your thoughts on the book would be extremely helpful in spreading the word to other readers (and this author would be immensely grateful!).

ALSO BY MARINA FINLAYSON

MAGIC'S RETURN SERIES
The Fairytale Curse
The Cauldron's Gift

THE PROVING SERIES
Moonborn
Twiceborn
The Twiceborn Queen
Twiceborn Endgame

SHADOWS OF THE IMMORTALS SERIES
Stolen Magic
Murdered Gods

ACKNOWLEDGEMENTS

Thanks to Mal and Jen for your speedy beta reading, and to Jen and Connor for your company and ideas on our plalks.

If you are wondering what a "plalk" is, it's a term my kids and I made up. A "plotting walk", or "plalk", is when we go for a walk and talk about our plots and whatever story problem we're currently wrestling with. Sometimes we discuss my writing, and sometimes theirs, but it's always fun tossing ideas around and gaining inspiration from each other. It's also a great way to sneak some exercise into the day!

ABOUT THE AUTHOR

Marina Finlayson is a reformed wedding organist who now writes fantasy. She is married and shares her Sydney home with three kids, a large collection of dragon statues and one very stupid dog with a death wish.

Her idea of heaven is lying in the bath with a cup of tea and a good book until she goes wrinkly.

Made in the USA
Coppell, TX
17 November 2021